MARGARET McGAFFEY FISK

Cover design, interior book design,
and eBook design by Blue Harvest Creative
www.blueharvestcreative.com

SAFE HAVEN

Copyright © 2014 Margaret McGaffey Fisk

This book is a work of fiction. The characters, incidents, and dialogue are drawn from the author's imagination and are not to be construed as real. Any resemblance to actual events or persons, living or dead, is entirely coincidental.

Published by
TTO Publishing

ISBN-13: 978-1-63139-012-8
ISBN-10: 1631390120

Visit the author at:
Website: www.margaretmcgaffeyfisk.com
Twitter: @Marfisk
Google Plus: MargaretMcGaffeyFiskAuthor
Facebook: MargaretMcGaffeyFisk

 Scan the QR code to visit the author's website.

OTHER BOOKS BY MARGARET McGAFFEY FISK

SWEET REGENCY ROMANCES
Beneath the Mask
A Country Masquerade

THE STEAMSHIP CHRONICLES
Secrets
Threats

OTHER NOVELS
Shafter

SHORT STORIES (eBook only)
Forged
War Child
Curve of Her Claw (Illustrated by Star Olsen)

CHAPTER

1

So, Madam, can you describe the mechanical?"

Henry Stapleton tapped his charcoal stick against a piece of paper, keeping the notebook angled away from the housekeeper. He'd learned, when he first joined the police force, where his uniform might not win him answers, the appearance of writing would.

After all, the staff had been trained for generations to bow before nobility, and only the upper class could write.

The housekeeper wrung her hands so strongly he feared she'd strip the flesh from her bones. "He'll blame us, Sir. I swear none of the staff put a hand on the cursed thing. Only brings the attention of Naturals, it does, having those contraptions in the house."

She leaned in close to add, "He thinks it makes 'im big. Important like. He goes showing it off to everyone. No wonder it's gone missing." She glanced around, features pinched as though worried she'd been overheard.

Henry swallowed a sigh. He'd joined the police force to help people in need, not track down rich men's toys. Some family legacy he followed. Though if it took the edge of fear from this woman and the rest of her staff, at least he'd have accomplished something.

Their master should be whipped for how he clearly treated those in his employ, but it wouldn't happen. The laws had yet to catch up to this new world where blacksmiths could put out steam-driven mechanicals and the new industry raised country merchants to the big houses. His father would have rejoiced to see this come about in his lifetime, if he'd lived, without noticing the troubles it brought.

"Don't you worry, Madam. We'll find your master's mechanical, and who's behind this rash of thefts."

"Thank you, Officer Henry. Thank you." She grabbed his hand and clutched it between her pillow breasts. "I can't tell you how much safer we feel with you about."

"Just doing my job." Henry extracted the hand and touched the rim of his top hat in a half salute. "I'd best get back to my team."

He'd gained a reputation as the voice for the small folk despite his bloodline, but hearing her, a soul would think he did so much more than take their word as evidence. His grandfather had hidden political fugitives. His father helped bring about laws to protect the weak. Just listening seemed too little an action to win such approval.

He turned away before his frustration caused him to lash out at the one who didn't deserve it, but she caught hold of his arm and pulled him back.

"You said a rash of thefts, Officer Henry. You don't think..." Her fingers tightened even more as she failed to bring forth the rest of the question.

A short laugh escaped before Henry could corral it. "Mum, we haven't seen a Natural on the loose in over a year, and never down here in these parts. Mechanical contraptions are expensive. Those that have them tend to wave the devices about just asking for them to be lifted. You said so yourself. More like some enterprising fellow is taking them up on the challenge and reselling the mechanicals for a steep profit."

She released him with a laugh of her own, one hand pressed to her bosom. "Oh, Officer Henry, I'm sure you have the right of it. The stories one hears are enough to send terror through the stoutest of hearts, but not yours. No sir, not Officer Henry. I'll keep you no longer. You'll find the fellow and bring him to justice for all of us."

"My team and I will have this wrapped up in no time," he said, squashing the inappropriate hope that this time it would be something more than just a common thief. He strode down the steps to join the other officers where they'd gathered in the street.

Catching a Natural would make a difference to more than just the wealthy. Naturals posed a real danger to the people with their wild contraptions running about harming folks. He'd seen them in the asylum—all new officers were required to do a stint there. Pale, wraith-like beings only vaguely showing their human beginnings.

That stint was the first time he'd left his grandfather's pocket watch behind since he inherited it. No metal objects of any kind were allowed within, but one of the attendants had been kind—or cruel—enough to demonstrate the reason behind the rule. Memory of those grasping hands and mewling cries haunted his dreams for weeks afterward.

"So, Sergeant, what you think it is this time?" Fitz asked, his words thick with the Irish brogue he'd shown no signs of losing.

Henry shrugged. "What else? A bunch of wealthy men showing off their contraptions to any comer." He glanced from one to the other of his five men, settling at last on Parson, a Scot from upcountry. "Tell me any of you found something more interesting."

They each waved their own notebooks, filled with random marks because none could read or write beyond their names, but those they interviewed never knew the difference.

"You know I can no more read those scratches than tea leaves," Henry said with a laugh. "Ken, what do your instincts tell you?"

Nicknamed for his ability to sense the truth behind almost anything, the skinny man looked nothing like a police officer, but Ken had better instincts than any other Henry had seen. Other officers had tried to pull him to their teams, but he'd refused each time, something that brought Henry a measure of relief.

Tugging on his forelock as though the night-dark strands held the meaning of the universe, Ken stared at the ground while his mind churned through the possibilities.

The others waited patiently despite the chill of late fall. Better patience now than wasting time Ken could have saved them.

Henry stamped his feet and wound his scarf tighter around his neck.

"Sergeant, it doesn't make sense. Not so many. What thief is so skilled, and yet so foolish, as to keep coming back to the same place?"

Ken's words brought a tension to every one of the six of them, the implications what an officer longed for—and dreaded.

Henry's heart beat faster. Here he could make a difference on par at least in part with that of his ancestry. Only a matter of time before the Natural started building mechanical monsters to terrorize everyone regardless of social position. The monsters got their name from a natural affinity to all things mechanical while their nature could not have been further from the meaning of that word.

LILY SMOOTHED away the wrinkles from where her fingers had clenched on her best skirt.

The solicitor continued his list of her father's debts, unaware of how his words condemned her, and condemned her sister Samantha most of all.

Mr. Cooper, Lily's employer and a friend of the family, shot her a concerned look, but she forced a smile on her face and tried to listen.

The solicitor paused to draw in a breath, his sunken eyes blinking at her and Mr. Cooper as though just becoming aware of their presence. "Now it's not as bad as all that," he said, rubbing his temple with one hand. "You have a good job and a place to stay thanks to Mr. Cooper here. I know it's not what you'd hoped, especially with having to sell your family home, but it's not like you'll be sent to debtors' prison."

Lily just sat frozen with her hands once again tangled in the rich fabric she'd never be able to replace, not here nor on the Continent where they'd been planning to go.

"Lily, you're a hard worker, don't think I haven't noticed in all these years you've been working at my bakery." Mr. Cooper sent her a kindly smile, a fatherly one when she had no father left. "I should have done this sooner, but there was the age to consider what with you being younger than some, and I didn't know what you'd planned once your inheritance cleared."

He paused, and the solicitor waved a hand as though to encourage him to go on.

They thought they had it all figured out. That the promotion Mr. Cooper had hinted at for a year now, even when her father still breathed, would solve all her problems.

"It's about time I spend less of the day at the bakery anyway, or so my housekeeper, Edna, tells me. I'll put you in charge of the place, with a reasonable increase in your pay, of course."

The solicitor clasped his hands together and grinned a little too enthusiastically, showing he hadn't been as immune to the impact of his accounting as she'd thought. "So it's all settled then. And a pretty girl like you from a respectable background, and with a good job, well, you should soon find a husband to care for you so you're not out on your own."

Lily rose, yards of cloth falling into place to hide her trembling knees. "Thank you, both of you. I'm sure I'll do just fine. I'd best get back to the bakery."

She was happy to hear the firm tone she used on the youngest of bakery girls issue from her lips. They meant well, but she could not take their kindness any more, not when they knew nothing of her sister, or rather both thought Sam had died at a young age. It had been the only way to protect her, but Lily never expected to face this alone. Her father had been healthy and strong despite all the troubles life sent his way.

Mr. Cooper laughed once. "As you see, she's already been in charge, and we all know it. I should have promoted you long ago, but never expected…"

His face turned the color it did when pulling hot bread from the oven, and his words stopped.

Lily put out a hand to brush his arm lightly. "I know you didn't, Mr. Cooper. None of us did. But you've been such a help in these past six months since Father died, even before that truth be told. He couldn't have chosen a better friend."

She swallowed hard against the threat of tears. She couldn't afford to give in to her grief, not now, and not ever. All their plans to take Sam to the Continent, to one of the few places she would be safe, destroyed in a single, horrifying moment. If only her father hadn't gone to Dover on business that morning. If only the carriage had held true. If only he'd been more frugal.

None of that could be changed now, so it didn't matter. She had to be strong for her sister. She had to figure out some way to fix this. They'd been counting on the inheritance, especially once it became clear hiding Sam at her lodgings was too risky. The abandoned stables Lily had found would not be comfortable once the winter's grip took hold, but now it would have to serve until the passenger ships started running again in the spring.

"He was a good man," Mr. Cooper said, clearly not for the first time. "We shall all miss him."

Lily stifled a bark of laughter, knowing it would take her too close to hysteria and be something she could never explain to these two gentlemen. A good man for sure, and a better father than any others knew. These two would have had him clapped in chains for the choices he'd made, her along with him.

"Come, Lily. Let's not dwell on what we can't change. There's baked goods to be tending." Mr. Cooper tucked her hand around his arm and turned to the door, his determined cheerfulness one of the things she'd always liked about her father's friend, a bright light in the gloom that threatened to swallow her family whole.

"Wait," the solicitor cried, "there's more."

Lily shivered, her body unable to mask the upset a moment longer.

"No, no." The solicitor rounded his desk, arms waving as though to wipe her fear away. "Don't you worry. Nothing bad. The debts are paid."

She focused on that fact with all her might, pushing aside the awareness that besides the single trunk of clothes she'd been allowed to take, everything else was gone. Every memento of her mother, every bit of inheritance from her father, the paintings, carpets, and statuettes that had decorated their home, all sold at auction. Even the toys she and Sam used to play with were gone, vanished just like both parents: one in childbirth and the other to a carriage accident.

"It's just I almost forgot what with all the bad news today. Your father had a single request about his belongings in the unlikely event of his early death. He asked that his journals be saved for you. They have only sentimental value I'm sure, not that I pried into his personal thoughts mind you, but they would have fetched nothing at auction."

He kept on about how little value the journals had, but his words became a blur as she tried to comprehend what he was saying.

Not until he placed the seven leather-bound diaries into her hands did she accept what he gave her. Tears sprung unbidden to fall on the top edges as she clutched this tangible piece of her beloved father to her. A sharp image of her father bent over these very books to record his thoughts came to her, a vision she'd seen every night as far back as she could remember. Within these pages, she'd find her father's voice restored to her and to Sam so they could keep his memory fresh and know him better even than when he still lived.

"There now, no need to fall to pieces."

The solicitor, when she raised watery eyes to look upon him, seemed flustered and actually backed away from her.

This time Lily did laugh, a small hiccup of sound as her lips spread into the first genuine smile since entering his tidy office. "Thank you for these. It means so much to have something to remember him by."

The man nodded twice, enthusiasm replacing a fearful expression. "Glad I could give you something. Sorry it couldn't be more, but what with his debts…"

Lily waved off further words with just her fingers, unwilling to chance dropping her father's journals. "No need. I understand better than you know. Thank you again for his words."

She spun for the door once again, but now her steps had more eagerness than weight. For the first time since her father's death, she felt close to him instead of abandoned.

CHAPTER

2

Henry nodded to each of the officers in turn, the situation fully discussed and a plan of action in the making. "So, we report this back to the station and start mapping out all the reports of stolen devices. If we can narrow down where to search, our chances of finding this Natural—"

"Or showing there isn't one," Fitz interrupted.

"Or proving none, are much greater."

Parson looked to add something more, so Henry waited for the Scot to gather his thoughts.

"'Ware," came the cry just to Henry's right, an unfamiliar voice breaking in on their serious discussion.

A contraption the size of a bulldog raced toward him and past as he dove out of the way, leaving Henry bruised and shaken on the cobblestones.

His men circled him, checking he wasn't harmed, but Henry shook them off.

"Follow that beast," he shouted at them, pulling his long legs beneath him and shoving upward. Ken had the right of it, as much as Henry hadn't expected so quick a confirmation.

The mechanism had a spider's eight legs, formed of metal joints and springs, allowing it to stretch and condense at an amazing rate. It ducked beneath shelves or skirted crates left in back alleys behind the businesses and houses faster than they could follow.

They passed Cooper's Bakery at a dead run, not pausing to draw in the delicious scents as they often did on patrol, rounded the edge of the dressmaker's, and continued down into an area filled with warehouses that bordered their beat.

Each time they lost the mechanical for a moment, the gap between them grew until Henry despaired of ever catching it. He knew just how many places there were for a thief to hide. How many of those would keep a Natural on the run just as easily?

Henry didn't slow, nor did any of the others. It mattered little whose area a Natural had infested when the risk such posed made catching it paramount.

"Sergeant, it goes in a straight path, or as straight as can be." Fitz leaned both hands on his knees as he fought to catch his breath. "Don't matter how it has to go. It finds a way."

Henry glanced behind them, mentally mapping the curves they'd taken and when the mechanical contraption ran straight down the path or ducked under drying laundry or through kitchen gardens.

"Good eye, Fitzwilliam." He scanned the way ahead. "If you're right, it'll spring free of that rain tunnel right about there."

Henry didn't wait to see how the others responded. He called on another burst of energy and charged after the one link they had to a Natural who'd already moved from cute toys to something harmful, intentional or not. The ache in his leg that flared with each step offered evidence enough.

He cursed whomever had failed to turn this Natural over to the asylums when the symptoms first showed. People thought it a kindness to give them a touch of life outside the asylum walls, and the asylums were certainly no stroll in the park, but a touch of freedom meant nothing to those corrupted souls. They lacked the ability to appreciate it and quickly devolved into trapped animals.

It had taken his stint at the asylum to prove this truth, but his grandfather once told him some people just couldn't be saved. This had shocked him as a boy, coming as it did from a man who'd risked his life numerous times to aid others, but full grown, he'd come to understand they have to want to be saved.

If Naturals truly belonged to the human species, they were one of that category—unsavable. No matter how good the intentions, nothing could be done to help them, and they could not control this curse even if they had the mind left to try.

"Ach, Sergeant growing too old already?" Parson teased as he bulled past Henry to take the lead.

Henry shook off his thoughts to focus on the chase as they passed yet another alley, making him wonder whether the Natural had gone to ground in a very different part of London.

With Fitz's realization, they'd been gaining on the contraption, eight legs or not. Henry kept half his attention on the cluster of grocery crates behind which the mechanical had vanished while he calculated whether they could get far enough ahead to trap it, or if they even wanted to.

A flicker of movement from the crates just as Parson charged across another alley opening caught Henry's attention. He slowed, focusing on the spot to the exclusion of anything else.

Henry thrust two fingers into his mouth and let out a piercing whistle as he'd learned from the herders on his father's estate. The mechanical had given up its forward momentum in favor of a sharp turn. They'd run it to ground.

He waited at the entrance to the alleyway, tracking it with his gaze, until his men gathered round him. Only then did they move forward as one, none willing to take on a mature Natural alone.

The mechanical slipped into a crack in the wooden wall of a shed not two houses down the alley.

Henry and his team approached more slowly. A glance at Ken showed the man's intent expression, proof enough their quarry waited on the other side.

The gap proved too small for a person, but only a foot further, a door hung at an awkward angle, one hinge missing. Not broken, but gone, most likely repurposed.

Henry waved one man to open the door while he and Parson stood poised to enter first, with the other two and the final man to follow after. Nothing in their training could prepare them for what lay on the other side of that dubious barrier. Encounters with wild Naturals were shared among the officers in hushed voices, half awe and jealousy, half fear, too rare for an effective approach to be known.

"Now."

His command sounded overly loud in the still air despite keeping his tone even.

The door swung wide, and he charged forward, police baton already in his hand, Parson similarly equipped beside him.

Whatever they'd expected, to be ignored had not been on the list.

A young man, naked from what little lay exposed, crouched half buried in a pile of metal pieces, some resembling known contraptions while others existed only in nightmare. Unholy concentration had taken hold of the man's gaunt face until Henry would have sworn the eyes in that face glowed, though it could have been a reflection from other gaps in the shed structure, the holes too precise to be the result of deterioration.

The pile shifted constantly as though alive, and Henry joined his men in circling it warily.

One of his men reached touching distance and moved forward to capture the Natural.

Henry couldn't believe it had been so simple. The stories shared must be ripe with exaggeration.

A hiss and groan sounded almost in the same moment as Henry's thought.

A contraption easily twice the size of the one that had bowled him over surged from the pile to engulf Peter, who vanished beneath metal pieces, his hand against the young man's shoulder the last to disappear.

"Peter!"

The cry came from all five throats as they pushed forward to rescue their friend and team member.

The Natural went mad, arms and legs lashing out in every direction, shucking any hold they'd managed even as more contraptions pulled free of the pile until Henry found himself fighting on all sides, unable to do anything besides defend. Some resembled the machines they'd once been, some he could not identify, and one even took the form of a little man. They all had a purpose in common, though, whatever their form: to defend their creator.

A roar from Parson gave Henry a direction, but not before he saw Ken dragged under as well.

When he reached the Scotsman's side, they went back to back, working in concert with the discipline they'd lost when Peter fell.

Together, they pushed their way through the wall of mechanicals, earning more cuts and bruises on the way, but keeping their feet as yet another officer vanished.

Parson stretched a long arm forward, and when he jerked it back, the Natural lay attached at the wrist.

Henry grabbed for his manacles at the same time as Parson went for his own.

In the chaos, Henry couldn't be sure which of them succeeded in making the sharp click as the manacle came together, but before they could capture the Natural's other hand, the manacles changed in front of them.

Henry faltered, his stomach twisting as he watched the blur of remaking underway. He swallowed hard against nausea and tugged his scarf free. The asylum demanded they bring no metal, even switching out belts for knotted rope. The scarf would serve better than any metal in binding this one.

Lost in concentration, the Natural didn't catch sight of him until Henry had one hand caught in a loop of tightly woven fabric.

"Parson, bind him," Henry cried, tossing the loose end to the other officer even as he held onto his side of the prisoner.

Whether Parson caught the scarf or not, Henry had no way of knowing because at that moment a mechanical surged free beneath his feet.

Henry toppled with a yelp of surprise he quickly swallowed before his mouth could fill with the gears showering around him.

They had no hope as long as the Natural remained to command his metalwork army. The men's lives were at stake, and Henry would not let lasting harm come to any of them if he could help it.

His fingers closed on a length of iron, and he pushed his feet through until they hit solid ground so he could pull free of the heap.

Henry had little time to consider as he rose in a clatter of scattering pieces. He saw a figure before him and brought the bar down with a solid thud, only then realizing he held a portion of a constructed spider mechanical with the rest twitching at the other end.

His ears buzzed with the lessening of sound though he hadn't noticed how it had grown until the mechanicals fell almost silent.

The Natural collapsed with a slow grace, and the mechanicals settled around him, puppets with their strings cut.

Henry dropped the length of iron, pushing aside a twinge of guilt at using the Natural's toys against him. A baton would have served just as well, but Henry's lay somewhere in the clutter, well out of reach.

Then the guilt collapsed too as Henry took in the chaos around him.

Parson lay unmoving on one side, the scarf still clutched in his hand.

Henry dug his way to the Scot, checking for any signs of mortal injury. Upon finding none, he turned to survey the rest of the shed.

Fitz dug at one side, pausing only to say, "Jim went down here."

Henry took the time to bind the Natural firmly in his scarf before joining the search. However the Naturals controlled their contraptions, they used their hands to build the things. If this young man woke before they'd passed him off to the nearest asylum, at least he wouldn't be able to craft new mechanicals to attack them.

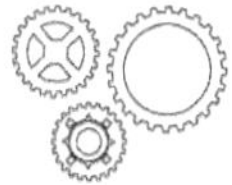

THOUGH MOST of the mechanicals had collapsed when the Natural no longer directed them, a few defended themselves viciously. Fitz and Henry fought them off as they struggled to free Jim from the rubble, but Peter remained lost. For all that the shed was no larger than a small bedroom, the pile of scrap metal seemed bottomless and held an unknown number of hidden dangers.

Peter had been buried long enough to suffocate had the mound been dirt, but the gears and metal bits left many pockets and passageways for air to reach even the deepest layers. Henry kept that thought foremost as he fended off another mechanical instead of shifting the weight from where he thought Peter might have been stashed.

A loud groan had them all twisting round and taking fighters' stances to meet the latest attack.

Henry caught on first and managed a laugh. "Get your lazy body up, Parson. We have Peter still to find."

Parson rose from the floor to shake his whole form, a scattering of metal parts showering off him to fall like rain. "Bashed me right proper." He rubbed the back of his head and glanced down. A laugh burst from him. "Looks like you avenged me already though."

"Enough with your chatter. Peter's still under here."

Fitz's sharp tone brought them all back into focus, and with the big Scotsman's help, they started shifting the pile against one wall, squirming mechanicals and all. A blacksmith would have to come and take the devices apart, or maybe Henry would bring his team back with sledgehammers. Either way, they could wait. Peter could not.

"Found him," Ken called from the other side of the pile.

The rest of them rushed over to help Ken dig their teammate out from under a weight of metal. Their efforts to shift the mound came undone in a mudslide of tinkling parts, but they knew where to look now.

Ken had found one black boot.

Working in concert, they began digging, the extra layers tossed aside with no thought to the noise they made.

Henry's ears rang with the clash of it as strong if not stronger than when all the mechanicals had been attacking. He didn't care, not as they unburied more and more of Peter with no sign he remained among the living.

As they cleared the last bits around Peter's cane-reinforced top hat, the young man sucked in a deep breath then exhaled and breathed again all before Ken and Fitz jerked him to his feet.

"Took you long enough to find me," Peter said, apparently unharmed.

Fitz punched Peter hard in the shoulder. "You could have called out. We were searching over there. Must have dragged you a bit. You'll be all over bruises, I suspect."

Peter felt along his arms and shook his head. "Not a bruise on me. The chill and my layers save me once again, though really it was my hat that kept me conscious. I couldn't cry out though. Not with the gears shifting around my face. I could only hope to stay still until you lot dug me out."

He shot an apologetic glance toward Henry who waved it off to say, "Speaking of those ever-loving layers, Peter, may I ask you to sacrifice one of them?"

The comical look on the young officer's face brought a laugh from Fitz. Henry could have been asking for the man's first born from that expression. Peter stood with eyes wide and mouth dropped open.

"But Sergeant, why?"

Henry pointed to where they'd left the bound—but naked—Natural. "Can't have the public see him in his birthday suit, now can we? Getting him to the asylum without incident will be hard enough without catching fainting ladies at every turn as they see Parson here without a shirt should he make the sacrifice."

Parson frowned, but the others burst into laughter at the vision of it.

"I'll have it cleaned for you when we're done."

That last broke through Peter's reluctance, and he stripped the long coat most only wore in the winter. "For the ladies," was all he said as they moved toward the Natural once again.

A wall of mechanicals rose to block their way, some as innocuous as simple wagons while yet others bore thrusting arms ending in sharp nails.

Henry ducked the first attack even as he heard his teammates do the same.

Parson threw several mechanicals to crack against the shed wall and make the whole structure shudder while Fitz kicked out their legs so they tumbled to the ground.

Henry couldn't see the rest as he reached for his baton. His fingers closed on thin air, the short length still lost.

A mechanical struck all too close, then faltered as it tried to get away, giving Henry time to grab two of its legs and pull with all his might. Just before he gave up, the joints snapped, throwing off the mechanical's balance and giving Henry not one but two weapons.

With a bellow, he charged forward, striking every mechanical within reach, but focused on his goal. They might have bound the Natural, but clearly he had regained consciousness, and with it, some measure of control over his creations. The only way to end this battle would be to remove its general.

Parson and Jim must have figured out his plan because they joined him in the forward offensive, turning the tides against wave after wave of constructed beasts.

Sooner than Henry would have thought possible, he broke free to stand almost on top of the man—or thing—sending this charge against them. He raised his makeshift weapons, but the legs were sharp. Henry had no intension of killing the Natural.

He tossed the metal lengths aside, only then noticing how a dead mechanical dangled from his waistcoat.

"Duck!"

Instinct had Henry react to the cry from Jim before even realizing his distraction left him open to a new attack. He needed to stop this once and for all.

He jerked the mechanical off him, realizing it had caught on the chain of his grandfather's pocket watch too late to stop the timepiece from tugging free of his pocket and arcing through the air.

Henry grabbed for it, his fingers closing around the gold circle before the eerie silence caught his attention, a silence that collapsed as soon as he'd regained his property.

He glanced at the Natural to find the man turning away to stare toward the mechanicals once again.

The pieces came together, and rather than safely returning the watch to its pocket, Henry let the chain slide between his fingers until the timepiece dangled in front of the bound Natural.

It took only one swing for the watch face to captivate.

Henry kept his attention on swinging the hypnotic pendulum, but if the changes in sound were anything to go by, his effort at distraction proved even more effective than he'd hoped.

"Fitz, bind his eyes with your handkerchief. That's how he's communicating with them, I think."

"He's communicating well enough now for even us to understand," Fitz said as he moved to comply with the command. "He wants your fancy watch."

Henry shrugged. "We must learn to live with disappointment. No one and nothing is taking my watch from me."

Thick linen fell over the Natural's eyes, and Jim and Peter stepped in to help hold the man so Fitz could secure the cloth.

Henry waited to see if the mechanicals rose against them once more, but the Natural seemed defeated at last.

"Bundle him tight. It's down to the asylum for this fellow."

Parson came up beside Henry as they headed for the shortest possible route. "Lucky you had such a pretty piece to bedazzle the madman, Sergeant."

"My grandfather watches over me. He always has since his passing. That's why I keep his gift with me on patrol."

The Scotsman grunted in response, superstition nothing new among men who tackled criminals and the insane for a living. "Guess you won't be using it to dazzle your lady friend then. You'll have to drag out some other heirloom."

Henry smiled and shook his head all at once. "First I'd need to find myself a lady. When would I have time for it, running about as I do trying to keep the lot of you out of trouble?"

Parson gave him a laugh for that, but they both knew the truth of it. Henry and his team went beyond the standard duties to ensure the safety of all the people of their patrol area. The others used their time after hours more wisely than he did, but still they had little time for courting.

Henry listened to the officers joking and teasing as they always did, as though they weren't shepherding a dangerous madman through the streets of London. His team might not be the most disciplined, but these men would do anything to defend each other, and they'd do anything to uphold Henry's principles.

The sound of the asylum reached them then, even before they could see the building isolated on the outskirts of town. The unholy howl rose from newer admits, Naturals or not, in Henry's experience, rather than those long kept as time sank them into an almost catatonic state.

Their prisoner had been quiet to that point, but now he began to struggle.

The team worked together to control him, all intent and serious despite their jollying a moment earlier. After the third time a blind kick or punch found purchase, they lifted the Natural between them to swing in midair with arms and legs trapped.

Henry waved Jim, the only one of the team left open besides him, to support the Natural's midriff so Henry could announce their presence. He accelerated his pace, wanting the asylum ready for its latest unwilling guest. He'd be happier the moment they passed this burden onto the proper custodians and could get back to protecting those without the means to protect themselves.

The whole business turned his stomach and left a sour taste in his mouth, but his grandfather had been right. He couldn't save everyone, and even had the Natural been an innocent once, now the young man threatened all the innocent folk who lived and worked in these crowded streets.

His team had removed a menace, one more of a danger than most, and his men deserved to celebrate that fact untainted by any twinges of guilt he might feel.

CHAPTER 3

Mr. Cooper handed Lily into the steam carriage, wealthy enough to have his own conveyance, but not enough to warrant footmen and a driver. The solicitor's office stood some distance from her lodgings, and horses had been largely banned from London proper in favor of the mechanical carriages to keep the streets clean.

"I'll hear no more of it, Lily. I'd send you home for the day if I thought you could afford it. As things are, you'll feel better with your father's journals safely in your room rather than having those girls dumping who knows what upon them."

Lily clutched the stack tighter, having already refused Mr. Cooper's assistance with the heavy books more than once. For all he teased, the younger bakery girls were less than steady. They required firm guidance to keep things running smoothly. It was little enough she could do for Mr. Cooper after all his help no matter how much she wanted to return to her rooming house and mourn again the loss of her beloved father.

She waited until he'd come round and hoisted himself into the carriage before protesting again, "There's no need. I've been away from the bakery too long as it is. The girls aren't as bad as you make them out to be, but Bettina will have her hands full with Jane and

Kate. And it'll take you out of your way after all you've done for me already this day."

Mr. Cooper fiddled with a few dials and then tugged one of levers down. The contraption gave a snort of white steam, shuddered, and began to move forward, guided by firm leather straps as though a horse stepped lightly before them still.

"My mind's made up, Lily Crill, and nothing you say is going to change that as well you know. I'll just visit with your landlady while you run them up."

Lily shifted to stare blindly at the houses going by, the white-capped servant girls rushing to and fro in this, a much more opulent neighborhood than the one she called home. She'd spoken truthfully about not wanting to put Mr. Cooper out, but she had better cause to keep her employer separate from her living situation despite her landlady being sister to Mr. Cooper's housekeeper.

Mrs. Marsh didn't tend to gossip, but when she had something to say, she'd never been one to hold back. Her scolds for the hours Lily worked had become almost routine. What else would they have to speak of beyond Lily? And too close a look at how she spent those hours would risk both her reputation and Samantha's safety.

She sighed, the sound loud enough for Mr. Cooper to glance away from his contraption and pat her on the shoulder.

"There, there, Lily girl. Trust in providence. It'll all work out somehow."

The reassurance offered little hope when fate would be as likely to turn against them. Considering what most people thought of Naturals, and with good cause, she had no doubt how they'd happily solve her problems.

Her mind drifted to her little sister. How Sam's face would have lit up at the chance to ride in a steam carriage, to explore its workings with the skill of a craftsman.

Somewhere there existed a very lucky young girl, the counterbalance to poor Samantha, one not sentenced by nature, circumstance, and prevailing thought.

"Off you go now. I'll be waiting in the parlor."

Lily's eyes focused on the present to find they'd arrived at the old townhouse she called home. "I'll be but a moment," she promised, not waiting for his reply as she unlocked the door and fled inside.

Manners would have had her seeking out Mrs. Marsh to welcome him. But manners could not hold sway. Every minute she could keep the two apart, the better chance she could get Mr. Cooper away from her house before questions were raised she could not answer.

Just as her second key turned the lock to her attic room, she heard Mrs. Marsh call out a greeting to Mr. Cooper, sending a spike of panicked energy through her spine.

The pile balanced awkwardly on one arm as she swung the door open, and the journals tilted a little too far. Before she could correct for it, the door bounced off her arm as it tried to close again.

Books flew every which way, some landing closed, but others with pages visible.

Lily bent to gather them up, grateful only none landed face down with torn pages.

She's my second daughter, the last piece of my lovely Violet. How can I bear sending her away?

The words caught Lily's attention and held it as she reached for the second-to-last journal. Her heart burned both with the sound of her father's voice echoing in her head and of the pain she shared, the wish for something different, some way to keep Samantha at her side.

She slumped, staring blindly at the journals in her hand as the revelations at the solicitor's office crashed over her. Her wish had been granted, and in the way of wishes, the result served both Lily and Samantha poorly.

A sharp laugh carried up the stairs and through her open door, reminding Lily of the need to be quick about this. If Mrs. Marsh got it into her head to check on Lily as she had the terrible day she almost discovered Sam, one glance at an open page could expose them.

Lily shoved her worries deep, swept up all the journals, and tucked them into her clothing trunk.

At the last moment, she extracted another key from her dressing table and secured the trunk. Lily never thought to need that key here, waiting for the time her trunk would be loaded on a steamship to cross the Channel. She hadn't expected to have something to hide.

But if someone were to come to her room when she was out and find the journals, all could be lost. If her father had given more than a quick mention to Sam, any chance, no matter how slim, of taking her sister to find safe haven on the Continent would be destroyed.

THE TRIP back to the station house passed in silence, the sharp rap of their boots on cobblestones the only evidence of their passage.

Henry didn't feel much like talking, but he hadn't expected his mood to infect the others. The station came none too soon, and he quickened his pace to bring them through the door as though returning to base would wash them clean of the sight they'd left behind.

The whole time they'd battled the Natural, he'd shown no signs of humanity, nor of sanity. He'd been a danger to be handled.

All that changed as Henry's team carried the Natural up the asylum steps to join Henry where he stood with the doctor, giving as best an explanation of the man's state as he could. Only then did the Natural take on a familiar, human expression: that of desperate fear.

With eyes gone wide and skin pale, the young man made a connection that Henry would have given anything to avoid. His discomfort grew to a fever pitch at sight of that face, and he could see it affecting the rest of his team as well. Bad enough they had to take down a Natural. Worst for them to feel a gnawing doubt about the treatment deemed proper for Naturals. Better to see them as something less than human.

"Home sweet home," Parson said, his long strides overtaking Henry the moment he pulled the door open and pulling Henry back to the present.

A deafening cheer slammed them as the six tried to enter the station. Gossip spread faster than fire through London, and their mad dash after a mechanical must have drawn more attention than they'd realized.

"How did you do it?"

"Were any of you hurt?"

"Did you collect any mechanicals?"

The questions washed over them, none of the team trying to answer them any more than Henry did as one query blended into another.

"Give them some room," came the booming voice of their superior, "And some tea."

In any other environment, Henry would have outranked every one of them, but in this, their inspector ruled with a firm hand.

Those gathered separated to let them through to the tables and chairs where the officers could take a rest and fill in their inspector on critical events. Henry and the others took this path and sank gratefully into chairs even as cups of tea appeared before them.

The inspector took a seat in the middle where he could look them each in the face, and more officers than should be in the station gathered around them to hear the tale.

Henry recounted it as clearly as he could remember, the others cutting in to confirm or correct some details.

It seemed no less fantastical in the retelling, nor did Henry feel any more confident in their treatment.

"Quick thinking with the cloth to bind him," the inspector said. "You were lucky to come through with only bruises and scrapes from what you describe. I'll give your standard beat to other teams for the rest of the day. You all report to the infirmary for thorough checks."

"But Inspector—"

Henry's protest came to an end with one stern glance from his superior. He could see the others were just as unhappy in being taken off the streets where they could do some good to linger here or in the infirmary with their thoughts.

"You've all been through something rare and disturbing. No matter how we try to prepare, the first unfettered Natural makes established truths seem shaky. Take time to process, or you'll be second guessing everything, and that leads to injury or death."

The inspector had no responsibility to explain his decision, but Henry appreciated the effort more than the order. He answered with, "Yes, Sir," and the others followed his example, if a few came out more as mutters. As much as he wanted to run from his thoughts, their superior had seen more than his share of conflict, and rarely had his advice steered them false. There'd be time enough to help those outside these walls. For now, his focus needed to be his team.

Lily straightened her room before heading back downstairs, taking time to compose her features and force back her fears. Still, she hadn't expected to find Mr. Cooper and Mrs. Marsh quite so chummy when she reached the parlor.

Mr. Cooper rose as she entered, the movement a bit too sharp to be without an eager need to escape the company. Before Lily could relax, though, he turned and said, "It's been lovely visiting with you, Mrs. Marsh, but there is work awaiting, and I have to get our Lily back to the bakery."

"Of course, of course," Mrs. Marsh replied, her voice a shade deeper than usual. "Can't keep any customers waiting on my account."

Mr. Cooper caught Lily's elbow then and escorted her out, restoring the impression that he welcomed the interruption until she realized it could mean he needed to speak with her urgently.

He said nothing as they settled into the carriage, nor once they started moving.

Lily's nerves wound up tight until she could bear the silence no longer.

"What did you speak of with Mrs. Marsh?" The question burst from her lips before she could swallow it back. If Mrs. Marsh had made him suspicious about her activities, everything was at risk. Better to know now than dwell on when he would toss her out on her rear.

Mr. Cooper stared steadfastly beyond the absent horse backs, a deep red growing over his visible cheekbone. "Nothing of consequence," he muttered.

Lily gazed at her employer for a moment before the pieces began to fall together. They'd been sitting much too close when she came in.

She'd thought conspirators, so trapped in her own worries, but a widow could have another reason to enjoy time with a handsome, available, older man. Mrs. Marsh showed much interest in talk of Mr. Cooper, even if the conversation most often concerned Lily's work hours.

"She's a spry, intelligent woman, Mrs. Marsh is," Mr. Cooper said after a moment, straightening on the carriage bench and staring relentlessly ahead.

Lily smiled at his turned cheek. "That she is. And of good heart as well. You did me a kindness in housing me there."

"Indeed." He coughed once, and curiosity begged Lily to push him, but as the flush faded, Mr. Cooper turned the conversation to flour sacks and sugar.

"I'll review the stocks when we get to the bakery, but I think we have enough supplies for now. Any more, and we'll attract rodents," Lily said, wishing her words better chosen as the last of the color drained from his face.

"We don't have rodents." His flat statement hid the question had not his pallor given him away.

"No, not so's I've seen, and the girls would have told me if they had."

"That's all good then."

When no more words issued from him, Lily let her thoughts wander over what she'd just learned. From his statement, she suspected he had developed an interest in Mrs. Marsh for all he seemed to put the landlady from his mind.

Lily felt confident his regard was returned in full, but how could she encourage him when he'd shown no intention of confiding in her, and she had no right to pry, especially not with the secrets she held close to her breast.

Still, surely a man of Mr. Cooper's years, having already buried one wife, did not lack in courage. Perhaps the differences in their stations stood in his way, though she suspected the fault lay more in inaction than intention. Mr. Cooper had only to say the word and Lily suspected she'd be out a lodging as soon as the rings were exchanged.

The steam carriage came to a halt in front of the bakery, but when Lily went to climb down, Mr. Cooper caught her arm.

"I know you've been staying later than you should, Lily. I didn't need to hear it from Mrs. Marsh when Bettina has mentioned it to me a time or two."

The tension she'd lost in contemplating a late-day romance returned with force, the base of her neck aching with the start of pain. "I like to get things set up for the next morning," she managed.

Mr. Cooper gave a slow nod. "And this is why I'm making you in charge starting first thing tomorrow morning. But today you had quite a shock. I want you heading home early. Get your rest and be ready to hold the bakery in hand all on your own. I'll deal with the closing this night, but don't expect me to do more than drop by on occasion after that. The bakery will be your responsibility."

"Yes. Of course. I will." Relief made her babble, but Mr. Cooper seemed to take it for appreciation rather than a release of the fear that he'd figured out she spent many hours elsewhere.

He laughed. "Go on and get down now. I have to take the carriage to its storage shed. Can't leave it here to block any fancy customers, now can I?"

Lily put a hand on the one he'd used to stop her. "Mr. Cooper, I can't thank you enough."

He waved her off. "It's nothing more than a good friend could do, and somewhat less as I suspect I get the better part of the deal. You are an efficient young lady. I do not look forward to the day some handsome fellow comes along and makes off with you. I'll be working twice as hard when that happens."

She swung down from the carriage bench, offering no reply to his tease. How could she when any suitor would discover Samantha? No, she had a comfortable position here at the bakery, and it would keep them well enough until she could find a way to get her sister across the Channel and to safety on the Continent. He would lose her in truth, but not to the expected husband.

THOUGHTS OF Mr. Cooper romancing her landlady were almost enough to distract Lily from her own sour prospects as she mended small disagreements between Jane and Kate, confirmed the stores, and prepared for the next morning's baking.

True to her word, Lily left before closing, letting Mr. Cooper secure the premises for the coming night. For once, though, she took the shortest route back to her lodgings instead of going to visit Samantha. She'd told her sister she wouldn't come and had made sure Sam had enough to eat.

Lily hadn't known how long the discussion with the solicitor would take, nor how much work would be waiting for her at the bakery. Little did she guess bad news would keep her away instead.

Until she figured out just how she would solve their seemingly intractable problem of needing to keep Samantha safe while Lily gathered the funds to take them to the Continent, she had no intention of dragging her sister's spirits down as well.

The walk gave her time to ponder, but the best she could come up with was finding a secret message in the journals that would explain where their father had stashed coins in case something terrible happened. His death had been unthinkable, yet perhaps he'd thought on the need to plan for just such a contingency. She could only hope.

"Back so soon?" Mrs. Marsh swung the door open when Lily started up the outside steps to her room. "Why don't you come in for some tea? Mr. Cooper is such a good man to take you to your appointment, isn't he? And to think he listened to what I said about how hard he works you." She paused, putting a hand to her still-brown curls. "Though I suppose that's for the best. He didn't breathe a word, but I could tell from his frown the meeting had not gone well. Sit down a spell, and you can tell me all about it."

Lily glanced at the outside steps, wishing she could ignore her landlady's request and carry on up the stairs.

"Oh dear," Mrs. Marsh said before Lily could start back down. "Just listen to me rambling on. I'm sure you're exhausted after everything you've done. Why don't you head to your room straight away? I'll make the tea and bring you a cup."

Lily gave her landlady a weak smile. "Thank you. That sounds lovely."

Mrs. Marsh made a shooing motion with both hands and stepped back inside the house, presumably to make the tea.

The steps had never seemed so steep. Lily's room had been converted from maid quarters at the very top of the house. She'd appreciated the room for its outside entrance, even if it had been a bit tight for the two of them. Samantha seemed happier with a stable to roam, and no need to keep quiet and still when Lily had gone to work. If only the winter chill hadn't already begun to creep in.

Lily didn't know how she'd keep her sister warm in the drafty old place, but the abandoned stable offered safety like no other location could. Horse permits rose steeply once the wealthy had a choice in transport that didn't leave manure on the streets. With only the self-same wealthy able to afford the permits, hire horses moved outside the city limits and many of those with money in city stables lost everything. The property had no value to attract new buyers so stood empty and ignored, allowing Lily to borrow it for her sister.

No day had seemed longer than one spent in the infirmary as he waited for each of them to be assessed. Fitz came out the worst, but considering what they'd faced, it felt nothing less than a miracle that bruised ribs made for the most severe injuries. None of them had cuts deeper than scrapes, and even Peter came through with a pretty face to show the ladies, as Parson was wont to say.

"We'll have our patrol back come morning," he told the rest as they were finally allowed to leave the station. "Get a good night's sleep, and set your mind at ease. The odds of finding another Natural in the next year are slimmer than Parson's wallet after a night on the town."

Parson gave a gruff laugh, but Henry could see something had the Scotsman unsettled. He hung back as the others scattered, waiting for them to be out of earshot before tapping Parson on the arm. "Have out with it. Such thoughts as paint your face will only fester."

"It's nothing much. Just unnerving how lucky we were. Like Naturals are all so dangerous, and that one sure seemed dangerous in the thick of it, but not a one of us badly hurt? And no reports of injuries from mechanicals in the neighborhood. Not a one."

Henry let out a sigh. "I hear your words, and I know them to be the truth, but it's like the inspector said. It's easy enough to let the cries of caged Naturals get under your skin. If we got off lightly, it's because we found him before he'd had time to gain full strength. That's the luck. You've been in the asylum. You know as well as I do that there's no human emotion to be found in them for all he might have seemed no more than a young man when we handed him in." He tapped Parson on the shoulder. "You'd prefer we'd waited until his creations attacked some child, or a young woman like your sister? You came all the way from Scotland to protect her when she married a Londoner. Don't doubt that today you protected your sister and handfuls like her."

Parson brightened at that, some of the gloom wrinkling his forehead fading away. "You're right. I know you are. And so's the inspector. Sure and I didn't expect it to be so easy to see the Natural as a man if you know what I mean."

"I do, but then how could we not. We're the ones who look at each not by station or position but as people. Why not one like him? And yet in this case, he wears the garb of a person much like the fae you mutter about when things go sideways."

A faint smile caught the burly man's lips. "Aye, like the fae. Soft on the eye and vicious once your guard's down."

Parson headed off at last, leaving Henry to stride in the opposite direction, toward where the streets grew wider and the stones smoother. He chose not to send a runner for his steam carriage or call down a steam hackney. The walk would give him time to convince himself as he'd done for Parson and the rest.

He'd no more expected the moments of humanity than any of the others, and seeing a young man in the Natural shook him at the foundation. Surely if there were another way, someone would have made it work. Casting Naturals into the falsely named asylums could only have been a last resort. He couldn't imagine a baron, or even a wealthy man, agreeing to give up his son if there were the slimmest chance of removing the Natural curse.

The thought reminded him of how, despite the world changing with industry, still most saw the underclasses as somehow less. The rules of bloodline maintained even when coin turned the inventive into a match for the riches of nobles. In some sour way, Naturals proved the only true equality. Regardless of station when born, Naturals were hunted and caged like dangerous, wild beasts. And he had the bruises to show the need for that treatment despite how it turned his stomach.

Desperate for a distraction from his thoughts, he cast his gaze around only to discover he'd reached Cooper's Bakery, a place with a grand reputation for delicacies along with breads and other staples. He'd never gone in, but often paused here on his way home to watch the young woman who closed up shop as late in the evening as he left the station.

Henry felt a kinship with her, both of them working into the dark hours, though she had no awareness of these moments they shared. He'd yet to speak to her.

He teased the others about their ladies in a good-natured fashion, but Henry couldn't see anyone of the fairer sex being happy either with his devotion to those less fortunate or his long hours. No lady he'd met in the years his parents still lived found his obsession, as they'd often styled it, appealing. He had little time or inclination for courting since being made sergeant of his team shortly after the packet ship sank with both his parents and his older brother aboard.

Sometimes, when his patrolling brought him down this street during the day, he stopped to watch the bakery girl laughing and scolding the others. She seemed a sensible woman, a hard worker, and she could not question his interest outside of his class, not when, as a shop girl, she stood among them.

Whether driven to gather fonder thoughts than those of the Natural, or just because the time seemed right, Henry vowed there and then to approach her and present himself. It wasn't as if he could wait until they were properly introduced. She did not travel in those circles, and he doubted he'd find one like her among the latest crop of debutants even had he the inclination to take himself to the lavish gatherings.

Besides, how could he expect the world to change if one such as he still held to the lines drawn between the classes? She would know him only as an officer of the law unless he chose to reveal his bloodline, and as such, would not expect such pretensions.

He took a step into the street to cross it just as the bell over the door jangled, announcing her imminent arrival. How he'd fold female companionship into his current, contradictory life, he had no notion, but with them both working long hours, at least she'd have no cause to chastise him for neglect as the last lady he'd attempted to court had done.

An older man, likely Mr. Cooper himself, stepped out, pulled the door closed, and locked it.

Henry's stride faltered at the sight, so focused on his decision, it took a moment to comprehend what he saw.

When he did, Henry let out a soft laugh and twisted sharply to continue on his way. He could wait until morning to meet her rather than appearing out of the shadows as though he would accost her for her purse or her being. He'd come early, before the bakery became crowded with its usual custom. With their reputation, he'd be sure to find all sorts of treats, enough to provide an excuse for his presence, and a reward for his men.

His stride lengthened, and a cheery whistle escaped from between his lips. Even with her gone, she'd served to lighten his mood. How much better would it be to know her truly?

ONE STRAND of blond hair caught between her lips, Lily turned the pages of the first journal she'd pulled from her trunk. Her father had detailed every step on the path to finding a safe haven for Samantha, who he spoke to, what rumors he'd heard tell of, and where he went on the few trips he'd made to the Continent. Had his solicitor not honored his wishes, everything would have been lost. He had been an excellent judge of character, though, and made firm bonds with those he trusted.

The letters grew faded and distorted, but when Lily blinked, she realized the cause came from tears, not any marring of the text.

He had not been perfect, but then what man could be? He'd had his moments of foolishness or bad temper. The loss of his wife had struck him hard. But Lily would have given anything to have him rage at her in this moment. To have him question her decision to hide Samantha away from her side, or persuade her to take her sister to safety even if it meant swimming the Channel in the dead of winter.

Anything but this.

His voice came through in his words so clearly it almost seemed he stood in the room with her, telling her all that he'd kept secret for fear perhaps that she'd misspeak, but more likely because he wanted her held separate should he be discovered. Better the ignorant child than a traitor and criminal in her own right for harboring a fugitive, or so he would have thought. Or maybe just that people would believe Samantha already dead from illness, freeing Lily to hide her sister no matter what judgment came down on his head.

The bedframe creaked as she shifted, trying to find a comfortable position when her discomfort had nothing to do with the soft mattress.

She had expected a life much unlike this one.

Lily's gratitude toward all those who helped her keep Samantha safe, knowingly or unknowingly, knew no bounds, but it shouldn't have happened this way. Her father was supposed to be here working alongside her. They were supposed to be heading to the Continent to find a place where the three of them could live in peace without worrying about the guard showing up at the door to tear Samantha away.

Lily brushed an errant tear off her cheek and stared down at the page, a page full of her father's hopes, and of his wish that there could be another way. The safe haven he'd found, the one he described within, would not have allowed them through the gates. He'd used up the money she'd been counting on to help others reach this place. She should have guessed that, should have known somehow that he would not have wasted his wealth heedlessly.

She wanted to rail at him, to thrust his foolish generosity in his face, to blame him for Sam's poor living space. She could not. He'd kept searching rather than separate their little family, never guessing what fate had in store. Had he any way of knowing what the future held, he would have moved them all to the Continent and continued the search there even though it meant leaving everything familiar for an uncertain existence.

A quiet rap at the door startled Lily, and she knocked the journal off the bed. "A moment," she cried as she scrambled to recover her father's writing and thrust it under her pillow. No one else could ever see those journals.

"It's just me. Mrs. Marsh. I've brought up the cup."

Lily grabbed her robe and wrapped it around her, pretending she'd been ready for bed as she opened the door wide enough for her landlady to maneuver through with the tea tray.

"I'm so sorry. I forgot you were coming."

"Tsk, tsk, my dear girl. You certainly had enough on your mind. Don't give it another thought." Mrs. Marsh lowered the tray, complete with a teakettle, two cups, and some form of butter biscuit, onto Lily's dressing table.

Lily glanced from the tray to her tiny room with only the stool at her dressing table for a chair. Mrs. Marsh would want to sit, and courtesy demanded she offer the older woman the softer rest of her mattress, the self-same mattress that held her father's journal, just waiting for curious hands to pick it up. Lily could see the edge protruding from where she stood, her hasty attempt to hide it a complete failure.

Seemingly oblivious to Lily's growing panic, the landlady kept up a stream of chatter as she poured out the rich black tea and added cream. She tucked a biscuit onto the saucer and lifted the cup to hand it to Lily.

Time had run out.

She opened her mouth, unsure what to say but knowing she had to say something to discourage Mrs. Marsh from settling in.

"Oh, you poor dear," the landlady said, putting the cup back on the tray. "Here I am rattling on when you're clearly too exhausted to have a nice visit."

Lily's mouth stayed hanging open in surprise for a heartbeat. Then she realized Mrs. Marsh must have seen her preparation as a yawn. She brought up her hand to cover her gaping lips and gave a rueful shake of her head.

"You've gone to so much trouble." The words when they came were not what Lily had expected. "It seems a waste not to enjoy the tea."

Mrs. Marsh gave a quiet chuckle. "You're kind to say so, but I'd be unkind to force myself on you what with you ready for bed and clearly needing its comforts." She turned back to lift the tray, but at the last moment, she took the cup she'd prepared for Lily and placed it on the dressing table instead. "You go ahead and enjoy your tea and biscuit. You can bring the cup down tomorrow, but don't take too long in drinking it or you'll nod off with biscuit crumbs on your chin."

As though to prove the landlady correct in her assessment, Lily smothered a true yawn behind her hand. "Thank you for the kindness," she said once she was able. "I'll have the cup washed and waiting for you in the morning."

"With what dear Mr. Cooper said, you'll be up and gone long before the rest of the house. If you haven't the time, evening will be soon enough. Or I can just come fetch it myself."

Lily helped the landlady lift the tray and carry it out the door, resting against the solid wood once it closed behind Mrs. Marsh. The last had been exactly what she feared. Her landlady would mean no harm, but how would she react to learn she was harboring the daughter of a criminal, the sister of a fugitive.

Lily would have to take the journals to the stables where no one would come across them by accident, and that meant leaving even earlier than she'd planned.

Rather than enjoying the tea and biscuit, Lily drank and ate them down as quickly as she could manage, knowing she'd need every bit of rest she could wring out of the night. She had a busy morning ahead of her, and that was without even considering it would be her first day officially in charge of the bakery.

CHAPTER 6

Sam, it's me. I've come this morning." Lily called out the warning as soon as she stepped through the stable door, knowing her sister wouldn't be expecting her and not wanting to cause a fright if Samantha had risen so early.

The sun had just started to lighten the sky, and the lingering chill of night made a ghost out of her breath. She adjusted the awkward bundle of her father's journals wrapped up in a blanket for her sister then bumped the door closed with her hip. The old stable creaked, and wind slipped in through many cracks that never warranted fixing when beasts inhabited the space, and had been neglected since.

The morning had seemed less burdensome when she slipped through the house to wash and return the cup and saucer Mrs. Marsh left with her long before the sun rose. The contrast between her life and what her sister suffered made her chest ache, but what choice did she have?

Past the outer room, Lily still found no sign of Samantha. She quickened her step, heading for the small tack room in the back where she'd made Sam as comfortable as she could manage without drawing attention.

As she crossed the hayloft, a creak and groan of wood boards made her jump back, stumble, and fall, her father's journals scattered across the floor. Hay showered down around her before she saw their source.

Samantha swept down the rickety ladder as though it were a grand staircase, or at least more sturdy than it appeared.

Lily swallowed both her scold and a sigh.

"You never come mornings," Sam said by way of a greeting. She thrust a hand down to help Lily to her feet, something aided by Sam's stocky build and Lily's slight frame. For a child, Samantha showed unexpected strength.

Lily could tell the moment Sam caught sight of the scattered journals.

"You brought me my books?" Her voice took on a reverent tone that, more even than the chill, sent a knife stabbing through Lily's heart.

Their mother had left a sizeable collection of leather-bound volumes full of fanciful children's tales, much more appealing than the learning books their papa had brought them. Some other children enjoyed those stories now.

"Wait."

Lily had time for no more as Samantha swept up the nearest journal and opened it not to the larger letters and beautiful engravings she'd expected but to their father's crabbed handwriting.

Her sister squinted in the dim light as the rising sun touched one wall and wove its way through the same cracks used by the wind. "What are these?"

Lily bent to collect the rest into a stack on the floor then shook out the blanket. "I brought you this to help keep warm."

Samantha waved the blanket aside. "The hay is warmer." Her words explained both the shower and the bits still poking from red curls.

"I'd prefer you use the blankets I've set aside. There's mold and rats in the hay."

"What are these books?" Samantha ignored Lily's request in favor of returning to the question of the journals, her limited reading not strong enough to work out the meaning, at least not in this light.

Lily tugged the journal from her sister's hands and put it with the rest. "Everything went to Father's debts." She'd meant to soften the news, but annoyance brought the words out in a sharp tone.

"Oh." Samantha seemed to shrink, showing she understood exactly what that meant. Suddenly, the journals lost the ability to hold her attention, and just as swiftly, Lily wished they still held Samantha. "What are we to do now?"

Lily grabbed the blanket and wrapped it around her little sister. "I need you to keep warm. Keep safe. Just for a little while. I'll figure something out. We will go to the Continent. I promise. It just might take longer than we'd hoped."

Looking every bit her eight years, Samantha gave a slow nod. "I'll do as you say. I'll keep warm and safe here with your blankets and the little stove. I'll be quiet, and if anyone comes, I'll hide away."

Lily forced a smile onto her lips even as the lightening sky warned her she needed to be on her way. "I know you will, Samantha. And now I need you to keep our father's journals safe as well. He speaks of you and of safe haven in them."

"Will you read them to me?" Samantha asked, her voice still soft and higher than normal.

"In the evening, I will. Now I need to get to work. Can you find a safe place for these where they'll be hidden and not even the rats can find them?"

A spark of mischief returned to Samantha's eyes, and this time her nod came quick and firm. "Not even the rats will find them. I'll hide them so well even you won't be able to without my help."

Lily laughed and pulled her sister in close for a hug, blanket, hay, and all. "I love you, Sam. Always remember that."

"I know, and I love you, too." Then as though the emotions became too much for her, Samantha dropped the blanket and made shooing motions toward the stable doors. "Now get to work. Bring me something tasty."

Out she went, her thoughts jumping from what awaited her at the bakery to her sister's request. Only if something burnt or was left in the week-old bin could Lily bring a treat, but she'd pray for fate to allow her this.

THE MORNING light had just started to reach a cloudy sky when Henry once again approached the bakery. A long night had done little to sway his conviction. He needed something more in his life than the seemingly endless pursuit of those determined to harm others. Even the camaraderie he'd found with the odd mix of fellows on his team failed to stop his soured perspective. Some days, he found it hard to feel any sympathy at all with those he captured, or worse, the sympathy sprung up where he knew it should not, as with that Natural.

He closed his hand on the doorknob and forced everything from his mind but meeting the young woman he sought. If nothing else, he had a reputation for catching those he went after, if in a very different context.

The bell he'd grown used to as a signal of her impending arrival this time announced his own presence, startling the only person he could see within.

"We're not quite open yet," she said while turning toward him.

Henry absorbed her soft voice, the tone more cultured than he'd expected. He knew it had to be her even before her face came into view.

"Oh," she said when she caught sight of him, once again startled. "Officer Henry."

He had his own turn at being caught. "You know me?" Whatever he'd hoped to use to introduce himself, such a weak statement did little to recommend.

A blush stained her pale cheeks, but she seemed to ignore it as she said, "Everyone knows you. The customers often speak of you and your team. All the good you do."

Henry seized on the reminder, and his excuse for coming in so early. "That's just what brings me here."

The color seemed to drain from her face as she took a step back and placed the counter between them. The move triggered Henry's police instincts for a moment, but he pushed it aside. He'd come here to have something beyond police work in his life, and clearly he needed the change if a shop girl moving to serve him better made him come alert.

"What can I do for you?"

Even her voice sounded fainter when viewed through his suspicious eyes. Henry scowled, and this time her flinch actually occurred, a response to his expression.

"Apologies, Miss...?" He let the question dangle, hoping she'd supply her name, but when she didn't, he continued, "I had no intention of disordering your morning. It's just that my men completed a difficult mission yesterday, and I thought to reward them with something sweet."

She laughed then, whether at him or her own reaction to his scowl he couldn't tell and didn't care. He vowed to provoke such a response again, and soon.

"We haven't much sweet this late in the season. The berries have all gone dormant for the winter, but I have some cream and jam tarts if that will serve?"

Henry leaned toward her. "These are simple men with few pretentions. They'd be delighted, especially if your baked goods are of such quality as I've been led to believe."

Again her color rose as she turned to gather the pastries. "This early in the morning, most are coming for the hot buns fresh from the ovens. It's a good thing you're not, though. The first batch is still baking."

He listened to the soothing babble of her words, drawing encouragement from how it seemed he flustered her. Henry had not planned to give up easily, but he looked forward to a smoother path in his need to know her.

"Oh."

Her change in tone brought him back to focus on the bag she placed on the counter.

Henry caught one of her hands where it fluttered around the edge of the bag, though he knew he should not. "What bothers you?"

She pulled away, shaking her head. "I never asked you how many you needed. I've probably given you more than you can afford."

"My men have large appetites, and there are sure to be others in the station should any not find willing hands. I'll forgive you the extras in return for your name."

She stared at him, once again appearing thrown.

Henry shrugged. "After all, you know what I am called. It seems only fair."

A faint smile played with the corners of her mouth as she dipped in as elegant a curtsy as any he'd seen among her betters. "It's Lily. Lily Crill."

Henry lifted his top hat. "It's a pleasure to make your acquaintance, Miss Lily. Henry Stapleton at your service." He gave neither his titles nor his police rank. She was to see him as only the man.

Her cheeks tinged a faint rose, but she kept her back straight as she returned, "My pleasure, Mr. Stapleton."

Only when her pointed stare remained did Henry realize what she waited for. He pulled a large banknote out and handed it over for her to produce change. She might have thought him checking her accounting, but he found her swift yet delicate movements fascinating.

"Here you are, Mr. Stapleton. Don't forget your pastries." She added the last when he turned to go with the change shoved into his wallet. They'd served their purpose, but he didn't want to make her question his motives in coming.

"It's Henry, Miss Lily. Just Henry. I expect you'll see me here again soon." As well she would. He hadn't lied about the men. They'd be happy to wolf down whatever he brought them, though he could already imagine the teasing he'd get bringing something so sweet to the station.

"Very well, Officer Henry. I'll look for you."

And with that he had no more excuse to linger. Henry made once again to tip his hat only to give her a half-salute instead. He did a sharp turn and used every bit of his precision to offer her a show she'd remember with him gone.

Henry expected he'd mull over this visit many times in the coming hours. Though it had some odd moments, overall, he felt the introduction had gone well. His hopes for a successful wooing seemed stronger than ever.

AS MUCH as Lily had to do throughout the day, and all the mock deference she had to suffer from the girls, her thoughts kept drifting to one fine figure of a man, one who had a mind for those who suffered as well.

She'd seen him on the street carrying out those duties often enough. How could she not when the other girls rushed to the window each time with inappropriate haste. Though she couldn't say too much about it when she followed after whenever she could.

For that very reason, she chose not to mention who had come in before any of the others arrived for the day. The teasing about how she lorded it over them was bad enough. To have Jane and Kate prying every detail of the visit from her as well as the focus on her promotion would have been too taxing.

Which didn't stop her from dwelling on it herself, or letting the event distract her from her labors.

At first she'd thought he came to arrest her, that he'd somehow learned of Samantha. His interest seemed too marked. Now, she wondered if she'd imagined it all. He'd done nothing so far out of the ordinary that she could point it out as proof even though her hand still tingled when she thought of how his fingers caught hold of hers. And he'd told her to call him Henry, though of course she had not—aloud at least.

"Are you closing up as usual, Lily? Or do you want me to stay late considering how early you must have arrived?"

The question jerked Lily from her woolgathering, and she stared at Bettina for a moment before the meaning could seep through.

"No. I'll be closing."

Had it been one of the younger girls, she'd have gotten a comment on her tone, something Lily regretted as soon as it left her mouth, too sharp for the question. Bettina, though, only put a hand on Lily's shoulder and gave her a light squeeze.

"You're clearly exhausted. You don't have to take on every task now, you know. Even Mr. Cooper doesn't do everything." Bettina shook her grey curls in emphasis.

Lily took the older woman's hand between both of hers. "I know I don't. You've been here much longer. Mr. Cooper should have put you in charge, not me."

Bettina pulled away and laughed. "You wouldn't see me responsible for those feather-brains for any amount of coin. I'd run screaming out the door before I let that happen."

This time Lily shook her head, the mop cap keeping her blond strands largely confined. "Well, then it's a good thing he asked me first. I don't know what the bakery would do without you here. You're a fixture at Cooper's."

"Hush now or you'll have me thinking you see me as the furnishing. I can easily lock the doors behind me and drop the key off at your lodgings." Bettina returned to the original conversation as though they'd never left it.

"And have your boys come after me for their supper? No, thank you. I'll take Kate and Jane over boys any day. Go on with you. Round everyone up and on your way. I have a few last things to manage then I'll be coming off behind you."

The older woman finally accepted the decision, much to Lily's relief. If any of them ever mentioned closing the bakery on the same day Mrs. Marsh spoke to her sister about how Lily worked too hard and came home too late, she'd have dangerous questions to answer.

As it was, by the time she got to the stable, night had taken a firm hold. Street lamps were common in the prosperous areas, but the gas globes were more widely spaced in places like where she hid Samantha. Lily stroked one hand along the wall, the side door hard to notice even with enough light to see.

Her fingers snagged, and she slipped inside quickly.

"Did you bring me anything?"

Lily started, pressing her free hand to her chest in a futile effort to still her pounding heart. "You're supposed to wait for me to call out," she said as soon as she could manage speech, searching the darkness for her sister.

"I could see you from my spot."

The rustle of hay gave a clue even before Lily's eyes adjusted enough to make out Samantha's climb down the ladder.

"So? Did you bring anything?"

Lily didn't know whether to laugh or sigh. Instead, she lifted the bundle wrapped in the end of her scarf. "I burnt the first batch. Good thing Mr. Cooper wasn't here today, but I'll have to report the loss either way. I brought my share of what couldn't be salvaged."

She'd asked for help in bringing a treat for Sam, never imagining fate would send Officer Henry to fluster her into making the error. By the time she'd remembered the buns, the ones on the outer edge had gone from an appetizing brown to coal black.

Samantha didn't seem to mind as she dug one out, though, and sank her teeth into it with a crunch. Through the crumbs, she said, "You don't usually burn them."

Even Sam knew something had happened, though Mr. Cooper might credit the error to finding her new job a bit overwhelming at first. Not that she had anything different to do, but now she had the responsibility in addition to the work. And look at how well she'd done.

This time the sigh won out. "No, I don't usually burn them."

"So what happened?"

She hadn't planned on telling her sister a thing about the odd morning visit, but unable to keep it to herself any longer, she found the words spilling forth.

"He's a good man, Officer Henry is," she said at last. "He keeps the streets safe for everyone, not just those with a title for a name."

"I thought you said he told you to call him Henry."

Lily felt a spark of gratitude for the poor lighting as heat suffused her face, but a quick chill followed soon after as she recalled the comments she'd overheard. Customers had been full of talk about the man's latest exploits. Her thought that he'd come to arrest her and imprison Samantha hadn't been all that far off.

Men and women alike were telling stories about how he and his team had chased a wild Natural to his den the previous day and dragged the monster through the streets to the asylum. Only luck kept her from having to respond to such talk on her own.

"Forget about Officer Henry," she announced as much to herself as her sister. "Bring out our father's journals. We can spare a candle stub to read the words he left us."

In the scramble to get the journals and set up a spot where no flicker of light would reach the outside, Samantha seemed to have forgotten the cause for the burnt buns. Lily was not as lucky. Her mind returned to him time and again, despite the danger, one made worse by each passage they read.

Their father had not been happy just to search for hope for his own family. The journals revealed once again how he'd gone through all their funds, as much spent helping other Naturals escape the constriction of England as he paid for word of elusive safe havens. Whether Samantha recognized the problems or simply enjoyed the sound of her father's voice as recounted by Lily, the journals offered neither hope of a hidden treasure nor a straightforward path to safety.

CHAPTER

7

Lily rubbed her sleeve across her forehead and stared around the bakery one last time, fighting the pull of exhaustion. She'd stayed late as she had every night since her promotion, and long before that if she were truthful. It began as a way to mask her visits to Samantha when hiding her sister in the attic room proved too risky, but the mornings ran smoother if she did a few extra steps before leaving. This made up part of the improvements that led Mr. Cooper to consider her promotion even before learning the daughter of his long-time friend had been made destitute.

She paused, her vision clouding over to replace the dimming evening bakery with this morning and Henry, who'd been true to his promise to return every day since the first. The girls were brimming with curiosity, but Lily said only that police work must make a man hungry.

Her lips curved in a smile before she hardened them into a tight line and set out to double check the banking on the oven fire. As punishment for her wandering thoughts, she made sure each of the flour barrels was sealed up tight as well.

Mr. Cooper didn't believe in the machines that were cropping up all over the place. Everything in the bakery was done by hand, from the kneading to the baking itself. She used to dream of bringing her sister here, something impossible even without Mr. Cooper believing Sam dead.

Now, she daydreamed of other things, other people. Most specifically, one good-looking officer who was perfect in every aspect—except his profession.

"Is the shop put up for the night?" Bettina called from the door, her cap freshly pinned against the stiff breeze of early winter. The weather had grown cold much faster than expected, and much faster than Lily's hopes.

A glance to the older woman showed all the girls clustered around the entrance as they waited for Lily's permission to leave. Kate, the youngest at sixteen, though Jane couldn't claim many more years than that, shifted from foot to foot, ready to burst out on the world, while Jane didn't even bother looking in Lily's direction, her hand already on the doorknob.

Lily gave them a smile. "It looks like you completed your duties well. Be careful out there, though. It's late, and the streets are icy."

The younger girls laughed off the warning, though they finished buttoning up their cloaks before letting the wind inside.

"You're not coming with us?"

Lily met Bettina's hard stare for only a moment as she struggled to smother a yawn. "I have some work still to prepare for the morning." She turned away so the older woman couldn't see the blush that touched Lily's cheek at the lie. "It won't take but a moment more."

A hand on her shoulder prevented Lily's escape into the back. "You work too hard. Let me stay this night."

Though she wanted to hug Bettina for caring so much that she made the offer every evening despite the constant refusal, Lily firmed her lips. "You have children to get home to. They're already waiting." She left Bettina to assume she had no one as they all did, though just for a heartbeat she wished she could confide in her, to share the burden of her secret.

Thought of how the other woman would react squashed the impulse as fast as it had risen, and she ushered Bettina out the door before the other girls, not stopping until her boot caught on the threshold.

The door swung wide as Jane and Kate rushed through as well, and a gust of wind made Lily shiver. She reached for the handle to close away the cold.

On the street beyond, a steam carriage ghosted by, the familiar clop of horse hooves replaced with a faint hiss of vaporized water and a ticking of gears.

"Make way, make way," a deep voice called out.

Along with the cry, the thud of mechanical boots gave warning. Those with coin to afford the many contraptions that skilled black-smiths produced nowadays rarely had a care for others who might be using the same streets. Lily supposed the warning could be considered a grand favor.

She stepped back to close the noise out with the cold when she noticed Jane had paused just outside the bakery doorway to admire the carriage and now stood in harm's way. Lily grabbed the girl's shoulder and pulled her to safety just before the mechanical boots carried their out-of-control owner clomping past the door.

A sharp whistle blew as the black-clad form of a police offi-cer ran after the mechanical boots, or rather the man using them to speed his gait. Lily recognized Henry as he passed. She doubted he had any chance of catching up to the fellow, but Henry would try. He always tried. New mechanicals appeared every day, and he and his team made a point of keeping the rest of the folks safe even long past the end of their shift. Even when the law would hold a nobleman above those who suffered, he had been known to intervene.

Oblivious both to the chill and Jane's presence, Lily watched him work. She didn't know whether to cheer or wince as the mechanical boots slipped on the icy cobblestones and brought their inconsiderate master crashing down. Her gaze lingered on Henry's impressive form.

"Come on, Lily. Let's go get a better look."

Lily laughed at the other girl's lack of fear despite her near acci-dent. "You go on. I have work to do." She might move closer to the window when he came by, but gawking in the street she could not excuse. Still, a tiny part of her felt proud of Henry, a personal emotion she had no right to for all he seemed unusually attentive when he came for some baked treat, waiting her out even when she found something to do in the back.

Bettina stepped away from the wall where she'd taken shelter, and sent a pointed look between Lily and Henry. "You should be getting on with your tasks, Lily. It's too cold out here even for admiring a young man's fine figure, especially with your cloak still hanging on the hook. He'll be coming in soon enough for next morning's hot buns. You can moon over him then."

Lily shook her head to deny the charge, a move that swiftly turned into a shiver, only proving Bettina right. She kept the protest trapped between her lips. "You get on home safely. I'll see you before sunrise."

Through the bakery window, she watched all three head out in various directions. If her gaze lingered down where Henry told the young gentleman off, no one could see but her, and once the others had left, she reached for her cloak as well. She'd done all the preparations already, but they had to believe she stayed later.

Lies built one on top of another, keeping her separate from those who would otherwise have become close friends. She reminded her wayward heart of the same. If she could not trust Bettina, how much more of a risk would it be letting Henry close? He considered hunting Naturals part of his responsibility to keep the people safe, and she didn't imagine he'd see Samantha as all that different, no matter what Lily would say.

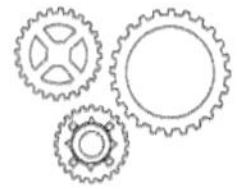

HENRY SAW the man go down with just enough time to slow before his own feet hit the icy patch. His superiors had suggested all officers adopt mechanical stride extenders to keep up with the latest wave of miscreants, but so far it had not become an order. Few of the men were willing to step into the contraptions because of safety concerns, and not just to the officers. Henry feared using the mechanicals would set the officers above the very people they were tasked to protect, or rather the ones Henry held his team responsible for.

Thought of the people sent his mind to the bakery, though it took little to provoke that effect.

He jogged the last few steps, keeping his shoulders back and his head up for an audience he felt sure included Lily. Despite his headlong rush, he'd caught sight of her standing in the doorway of Cooper's Bakery, and the tingle at his back made him suspect she watched him still. The morning couldn't come early enough, the highlight of each day a few short words exchanged over hot bread.

Henry dragged his mind back to the situation before him, the image of a blush brightening Lily's cheeks or a glimpse of her shy gaze too distracting when he needed to focus on bringing this man down to the station for the next shift to deal with.

He came to a halt beside the man who thought so little of endangering the walking folk, and his smile vanished into a severe frown. His fingers closed around the man's shoulder with perhaps more force than necessary, but Lily could have been among those walking home after a long day.

The quality of the fabric beneath his chilled fingers might have given another officer pause, but Henry had no such inhibitions toward those of wealth and position. "You are in violation of Ordinance 15 of the Mechanical Laws, my good sir. It states clearly that you are not to venture into populated parts while making use of a mechanical you have not attained mastery of." The law came into being to protect property more than people, but it had its uses.

"I had full control," the man muttered. "Not my fault there's ice on the roads. You have some fancy law to cite against Nature, too?"

Henry recognized a hint of Oxford in the man's tones, and his scowl deepened even as he lowered his estimate of the man's age. "I'd expect nothing less from an Oxford student," he said, emphasizing the Cambridge edge in his own voice to show he could not be bullied. "Full control does not mean barging through with little thought or care for those endeavoring a more mundane form of loco-motion. Remove those mechanicals from your feet, and we shall see if a stroll down to the station puts you in mind of how you should have behaved."

He gave the young man a shake, keeping his grip even as the other bent to remove the offending boots, though he refrained from giving a shove to speed the process.

Henry glanced over the man's shoulder now that he had the situation under control, but Lily had gone. He squashed the disappointment. With his body cooling off after the exertion of his run, the chill wind teased his neck above the heavy wool of his police coat. He could hardly have expected her to wait long in this inclement weather. It was enough that she paused at all.

She'd proved more reticent than he'd expected, growing more skittish than a filly in first heat whenever he approached. Still, he'd worked with enough animals on his father's estate to know sometimes the most nervous required little but a firm hand. Where subtle wooing had no noticeable effect, a request to step out with him might change her sideways glances into a direct smile.

Frozen slush crunched under her serviceable boots as Lily headed off to visit with her sister, leaving the bakery and Henry behind. Winter had come upon the town for sure, and it looked to be a bad one. Some of the older customers blamed the main steam engines, saying the coal dust drew down the clouds. Despite crafty filters and wind-up devices like the mechanical boots that absorbed their charge elsewhere, Lily still got a gritty aftertaste whenever one of the machines passed her. Or maybe her teeth ground because of Samantha.

If only Mrs. Marsh hadn't overheard Lily talking to Sam in late summer when her sister still lived in the attic room. Only the stable made bitter weather so important, but discovery meant losing her lodgings and her job, at the very least. The worst meant Lily jailed and Samantha thrown into the asylum.

Lily shuddered, though not from the cold. She'd heard stories of the place but had never ventured close enough to see for herself.

They had to make it through the winter now. With the weather gone so cold, all but the packets had stopped traversing the Channel, and Lily didn't have enough to buy passage anyway. Even were the passenger ships still running, Mr. Cooper would never give her a reference based on whatever wild story she could come up with so she could work her way across. He might have been persuaded if she had a grand inheritance from her father. As it was, he thought of her as his daughter and would never allow her to run off to the Continent with no prospects.

He deserved better than for her to vanish without word, but she had to think of Samantha first. When the weather broke, she'd find a way whatever she had to sacrifice, including Mr. Cooper's good will, though it seemed a poor way to repay his kindness.

The hiss of a steam coach, rare this close to the stables, pulled at Lily's attention.

She turned to watch it move down the last street before the alley, remembering Jane's near accident though boots were much a different prospect than a coach, steam driven or not.

The driver appeared to be the cautious type and posed no risk to her. Still, a mechanical device so close to Samantha brought with it other problems. Responsible masters or not, how could she keep her sister safe with gears whirling outside every door?

The mechanical boots that had almost bowled poor Jane over could have used transformation into something less hazardous.

Lily pushed the thought away. A blacksmith might improve the design. What Samantha would do there was no way of telling. She'd be as likely to transform the boots into something completely unexpected like a rolling cart or a child's toy, as Naturals were wont to do regardless of the wishes of those who owned the expensive devices.

Talk as much as people did about how Naturals made dangerous contraptions, Lily knew the heart of the brutal Natural laws lay not in any person's safety or all the machines would be banned from London and even England itself. No, the purpose behind locking up Naturals with a knack for the new machines had little to do with protection of people and everything to do with the desires of those with enough coin to afford more and more complicated devices.

Lily drew to a halt in front of the stable. At least the acceptance of machines brought them this shelter.

She knelt as though to retie her bootlaces next to the weathered wood, once gay paint faded and peeling. From her crouch, she checked up and down the street for any watchers, but the shutters were all secured against the cold night, and the few walkers like herself were too distant to take note.

The stable offered safety in its general sense of neglect. Should any suspect a resident, though, the investigation would reveal more than they'd expected, and just what Lily would do anything to prevent.

Lily rose as though to keep going, but at the last possible moment, she ducked into the tight alleyway that ran along the stable's side. Her work-hardened fingertips found the ridge marking the side entrance latch by habit though enough light remained for her to see.

Once inside, the stable welcomed her. Faint illumination from distant gas globes hid the interior's wear from view while the discarded hay trapped heat both from the weak sun and the small woodstove she'd found for Samantha to use only if it shed no light outside. Lily shucked her cloak near the entrance, the contrast with the outside air making the stable seem much too warm.

Habit, too, had her straighten both her back and her dress, smoothing away wrinkles to present a tidy appearance despite the dusting of flour her apron had failed to contain and a shiny spot on her sleeve where she'd brushed too close to a honey-glazed pastry. Samantha could never know how much it cost Lily to keep her sister safe, especially now when they could not count on a tidy inheritance to restore their old comforts.

"Lily! You're here."

A creak then rush of wind was the only warning as Samantha landed in a puff of dust, the rope she'd used to launch from the hayloft twisting in the dark in counterpoint to a groaning pulley. She hadn't even bothered with the ladder.

Lily swallowed her scolding. Samantha could have hurt them both, but she had so little to amuse her locked in the empty stable day and night. Then she remembered the steam coach so close and grabbed her sister's shoulders, giving Samantha a firm shake. "You mustn't act so. You must remain hidden even here. It's much too dangerous."

The effort made little impression as Samantha laughed. "I knew it was you, Lily. I wouldn't have come down otherwise. Even if I couldn't see you in the shadows, who else would smell of fresh-baked bread?" She sniffed hard, breathing in the yeast scent that clung to Lily no matter how much she tried to wash it off. "And you made cinnamon buns today. Tell me you brought me one. Tell me."

Lily pulled her sister into a close embrace.

Samantha let the hold continue for longer than usual, perhaps not as oblivious to the danger as she seemed, or maybe only aware of Lily's worry.

A moment more passed before the little girl twisted away. "I am hungry, Lily. The root barrel is almost empty and what remains is starting to blacken. Please say you brought food. I promise not to complain if you didn't bring me a sweet bun. I promise."

Wiping back a strand of red hair, so unlike her own blond, Lily smiled at her sister. "Of course I brought food. Both to share and to keep you while I'm not here. It's in my cloak pockets."

No sooner had she spoken than Samantha raced to the discarded cloak and pulled out three packages wrapped in brown paper. "Come on then."

Lily followed after her grinning sister, the delight in packages that contained only tough ends of butcher sausage and week-old bread as endearing as it saddened her. Even if they could use the stove to cook something here, the smell would reveal them. Enough wood burned in the area to stave off the cold for the stove itself to pass unnoticed, but they couldn't risk more than that.

Sometimes Lily cooked a little extra in Mrs. Marsh's kitchen, but if she did it too often, her landlady would start to ask questions Lily couldn't answer, even if the assumptions from a stronger-than-expected appetite would harm her reputation faster than revealing the truth. Even before moving to the stables, most of Samantha's meals had been, of necessity, cold.

Lily reached the tack room doorway and glanced around as she pulled the door shut behind her.

Samantha had already passed through and begun to spread their meager feast on the table, but the object taking up the same space where a stove had been just this morning made Lily pause. "Oh dear." The words held none of the force of her reaction, but it was all she could get out.

Lily looked from the device to where her sister had frozen with a guilty expression on her face. "Samantha," she began, trying to come up with the right thing to say even as she spoke. "I know I shouldn't have tempted you. I shouldn't have put even so simple a metal piece in here with you, but it's all that keeps you warm." She turned to stare at the odd-shaped object, wondering what it was supposed to be. It held little resemblance to anything Lily had seen before, but judging from the warmth in the room, Samantha must have dismantled the stove recently. Perhaps she was still working on it.

"It's not what you think, Lily. I swear it's not."

Her sister's adamant tone made Lily turn back to see the contrition vanish into an all too familiar look, eyes wide and bright as though Samantha, not her creation, were wood-fired.

"I made it better. It's still a stove, just like you gave me. It's just a better stove." Samantha grinned and rushed over to the object. "See, I took this—"

Lily let her sister's description wash over her, the process by which Sam talked to the objects to learn what they wanted and how to do it something well beyond her comprehension.

The transformation had done exactly as Samantha said. Lily had recognized the stable's warmth from the moment she entered.

Part of her marveled at what her sister had done, much like her own thought about the mechanical boots, but she kept a firm grip on her disapproval. In another world, another lifetime, maybe Naturals like Samantha could harness their innate talents to improve the mechanicals that were invading every aspect of life, but not in this one. At least not here.

Here, Samantha's affinity to all things composed of moving metal parts made her sister a fugitive and Lily her accomplice. The law was clear. All Naturals must be confined, trapped away from where they might harm society. Looking at the stove, once again Lily thought convenience for the wealthy lay behind the law, not true safety. What industrialist wanted a Natural to come along and improve what a person already had rather than making the person purchase something new? No, if Naturals were allowed freedom, those with means would hunt them down and cage them with another excuse.

Samantha met Lily's gaze in that moment, and her excited recitation faltered. She stared at the ground, one shoe-clad toe twisting in the scatter of hay covering a packed dirt floor. She must have been cold, indeed, to wear shoes. "I'm sorry, Lily. Truly, I am. I tried as hard as I could to resist, but it got colder today than ever before. I couldn't stand the chill, and the stove wanted so much to be able to keep me warm."

Lily dropped to her knees, pulling Samantha tight against her. "I know, Sam. If I could give you anything better, I would. I want you here in this drafty stable no more than you do, but there's no other choice. Even had we the money for tickets, the passenger runs have ended for the winter. We'd stand out too much on a packet. You just have to stay hidden for a little longer. I can't—I won't—lose you to an asylum."

Samantha leaned hard into Lily's shoulder, her own body shuddering. "Maybe you should," she whispered, her childish voice even higher than normal. "Maybe you should give up on me. Then you could live a normal life, a life like you had with Father and Mother before I came and spoiled it all."

Holding her sister at arm's length with a hand on each of the little girl's shoulders, Lily waited until Samantha looked up to frown. "Now I won't hear any of that talk. This is the life I choose. The life I want. You mean more to me than any other. It would kill me to see you locked away."

She waited again until Sam lowered her head in a nod before continuing. "Just tell me you'll be careful. That you'll stay inside no matter what, and you'll leave the stove alone from now on. If you're cold, I'll bring more blankets. If you're lonely, I'll make you another doll, or maybe an animal this time. I promise I'll do my best to make this place a good home for you until we can leave. Just promise me you'll stay hidden. That you won't take any chances."

When Samantha tried to look away, Lily gave her shoulders a quick shake. "Promise me, Sam."

Samantha raised tear-filled eyes to look at Lily. "But it's not fair to you."

Lily forced a laugh. "And this is your idea of paradise, little sister? But we make do with what we're given. I don't care if it meant I could sup at the Queen's own table. I wouldn't give you up for anything. You understand?"

"I understand. And I promise I'll try harder."

Lily had to make do with the quiet whisper. Samantha had too much weighing her down as it was, pressure that both made her older in some ways and much younger in others.

"Well then, weren't you hungry? Positively famished?" She injected cheer into her tone as she deliberately turned her back on the remade stove. She had to admit it produced more heat than the old one ever had. "I brought some more bread and sausage ends. With the last of the root vegetables, you should eat well."

Samantha tapped Lily on the arm as she moved to the table. "I'll eat like a queen."

Lily appreciated the effort, though it only emphasized what little of a life her sister could claim.

"Tell me about the machines you saw today."

The demand came with a spray of crumbs, and Lily put aside her own meal to shake her head. "You know better than to behave so poorly. You're not a savage."

Samantha pouted for only a heartbeat before swallowing so she could ask again, "What mechanicals did you see? Please, Lily. Tell me everything. It can get so tiring locked up in here."

Never able to hold firm against her sister's pleading, in part because she should have been able to do better by Samantha, Lily trotted out the story of Henry's grand exploit. She told how he caught an arrogant man who cared little for those he trampled with his mechanical boots.

"What I could do with boots like those." Samantha propped her head on folded arms and stared blankly at the wall.

"This is exactly why I don't tell you about the machines I see. It does no good and only makes your cravings worse. Look at what you did to the stove."

"I made it better." The pout had returned.

Lily didn't want to concede the point so changed the topic back to her story. "You missed the purpose of my tale, Sam. Mechanicals are dangerous, even those made by simple blacksmiths. If not for men like Henry to protect us, who knows how many would be harmed each day."

"It's not the mechanicals. It's not their fault. They don't want to harm anyone."

Lily stared at her sister, stomach churning until she regretted the few bites she'd managed to consume. "How would you know?"

Samantha looked down at her twisting fingers. "They come sometimes." Her head came up and her voice quickened. "I don't let them in. I swear I don't. It's just I can feel them, feel what they want."

Lily sank her head to the table, its weight too much to bear. How could she protect her sister if mechanicals came knocking? Samantha wouldn't need to do a thing, and they'd still be revealed as people questioned the gathering.

"I told them to go away, Lily." A soft hand rubbed her cheek. "I told them to go away and pass the word to others. You don't have to worry. Most will listen."

Lily raised her head only to shake it. "They're just gears and springs with steam to drive them, Sam. I don't understand this. How could they seek you out? How do they know?"

Samantha shrugged, returning to her side of the table and the remains of her meal. "I don't ask. I know you don't want me to, truly you don't."

Lily shoved her plate over to Sam, unable to eat another bite. "You can have the rest of mine. I'm done."

Whether peace offering or simple truth, Samantha was never one to argue about food, and this time proved no different.

Lily went to where Sam had hidden their father's journals and started reading where they'd left off. She had sewing to work on. Samantha grew at a good rate despite her confinement, and it was all Lily could do to keep the girl's ankles covered and arms warm. But for now, she needed the comfort of their father's voice, even if the words themselves told only of failure. Failure to find a safe haven where they could all live, and failure to set aside the funds they needed to get there.

HENRY ROLLED his shoulders and sank into an armchair. The fire crackled merrily, started by the maids to warm his study for when he returned. He lifted his glass to admire the rich brown liquid within it before taking a light swallow.

The other officers out of his station went home to small quarters and spent their time out at taverns. He could appreciate the irony of coming home to be waited on hand and foot at the end of a long day looking after folk little different than those who staffed his London townhouse.

Still, many of his employees had been here since before his birth. Whatever concerns he might have about the lines drawn based on bloodline, he wouldn't use his convictions for harm.

"Here's your repast, my lord."

He turned to smile at Bessie, a dark-skinned woman his father brought home from one of the merchant voyages. She'd wanted to see the world. Henry wondered if working in London offered what she'd hoped when she left her small village on the coast of Africa, but he'd never heard a complaint, and she'd been here longer than he had.

Cook had made sandwiches—thick pieces of bread, slathered with butter, and meat between. They'd come to this agreement when Henry proved incapable of arriving at a consistent time. The cold meal seemed odd at first, but he'd grown used to it.

These little accommodations left him with a happy household staff. They didn't feel as though they shirked in their labors, and he didn't have the pressure to be a proper lord. It had never been his plan. His brother had the firm tone and ability to make an argument sound reasonable even when it twisted expectations. Where Henry upheld the law in ways to protect those normally beneath notice, Robert had worked to change that law. When Henry tried, he met barriers stronger than the stone walls of the Tower of London itself. Convincing others had never been his forte, and he had little interest in developing the skill. He preferred the more active approach.

Henry's mind turned to his latest pursuit, not of a criminal out to harm but rather of the most enticing female he'd had the pleasure of sharing company with. Had she been a woman of society, he could take her riding in the gardens, but suggesting anything to do with horses would only reveal his station in these times of hefty permits.

He kept his title secret, though his men knew of course, more because it set him apart from the people he protected than because of any nefarious purpose. With Lily, though, he didn't want to discover she sought the chance to change her station more than having particular interest in him, nor would the knowledge make her any less skittish around him. After all, his intentions toward a shop girl as a lowly police officer seemed simple. For her to learn of his title would make every approach suspect.

Henry shifted until his elbows rested on both knees, staring into the fire as though its dancing flames could offer an answer to his tangled thoughts. He had no one else he could ask about the appropriate outing for one of her class. The servants would be likely stunned at the query, and his own men just might be the first to question his intentions.

The concept would be so much simpler if he understood his own motives beyond the need to have something greater than his job.

Lily intrigued him as no woman had before, not in society or outside of it. While he could not imagine her agreeing to be his mistress, nor did he want that of her, Henry wondered if he'd be punishing her with the demands of his class should he seek a more permanent state. She had the commanding tone and ran the bakery much like a lady wife would run a household, or so he supposed, but society itself would be alien to her and it could be unkind to outsiders.

The fire did not care that he scowled as he considered how everything that drew him to Lily could be seen as no more than a nobleman looking for a dalliance where the expectations were low. This, as much as anything, proved why he kept his title hidden, but just how long did he think to dangle after Lily while keeping a secret of more magnitude than any she must have faced in her life. How long could he let her spin fairy tales of their future, never knowing what she'd be committing herself to?

A tongue of yellow, orange, and white danced along one of the logs and provided both a distraction he desperately needed and a solution to the outing. He would take her to Covent Garden Market to look at the flowers in the new glassed-in market street.

Scowl as he might, question his own motives as well, something about Lily drew him stronger than a magnet pulled on iron. He'd just have to figure out what to do next when that day came.

AS MUCH as she wanted to stay with her sister, Lily soon tucked the journal away, kissed the top of Samantha's head, and ventured back out into the cold.

The games she played to keep this secret terrified Lily. She had only to think of how much she learned from the customers to know rumor and gossip were the main repast of Londoners from all stages in society. One misstep, one hint that all was not as it seemed, and they could lose everything.

Mr. Cooper would have to cast her from her job should rumors start that living on her own without parents made her forget proper behavior. His loyalty to her father's memory meant little when measured against the bakery and his own reputation.

These dreary thoughts plagued her as she drew out her key to open the main door of what had once been a single dwelling much like the home she'd grown up in, now sold to pay Father's debts. She hadn't the strength to fight the wind on the outer staircase to her room.

"Lily, girl. That you coming in so late? Mr. Cooper works you much too hard." Mrs. Marsh came out of the kitchen just as Lily started up the four flights of stairs leading to her room. "Come sit a spell. You can have the rest of the soup I made for dinner. I made too much and there's no need for it to go to waste."

Lily shook her head, too tired to pretend. "Thank you kindly for the offer, but I'm not hungry just now. I'm off to get some sleep."

"I'm half a mind to march uptown to speak to that man. It ain't right what he expects of you."

"Please, Mrs. Marsh, don't do so on my account. I need the job, and I'm happy to do my best for him. He's been a good friend to my family. He doesn't ask this of me. I choose to do it."

The landlady's stiff back eased at that, a faint blush taking up residence in her plump cheeks. "Right you are. He is a good man. Got you this place, didn't he?" She leaned in close, her eyes sparkling as she spoke of Mr. Cooper. "You must know well enough I wouldn't have taken in a single female like yourself without strong references."

Lily stifled a yawn. "Well I know it." Her own thoughts about the need to seek a shipboard position had reminded her recently enough. Still, knowing what she now did about the affection between Mrs. Marsh and her employer, she enjoyed relieving any concern the older woman might have. "It's why I work so hard. A lifetime of long hours couldn't repay the good he's done for me since my father's death."

"So unfortunate a happening and to such a nice young woman." Mrs. Marsh patted Lily's shoulder twice then gave her a nudge toward the stairs. "Well, then, don't let me keep you, tired as you are. Head on up and rest well."

Lily could feel her landlady's gaze on her as she mounted the steps, grateful the woman had accepted her explanation for the late hour. As long as she did nothing else to raise questions, she might just manage to tend to Samantha without provoking dangerous attention.

"Now that girl barely eats enough to keep a bird alive."

The mutter reached Lily just as she moved to the second flight.

How she longed to tell the truth about where she ate and the life she led. Lily had always been an honest, truthful person about everything except her sister, but never had so much hung in the balance. She heard the warning in her landlady's comment, though she felt sure the woman meant nothing by it. Anything out of the ordinary could prove deadly. She shuddered to consider what they would do if ever they discovered that her sister, rather than dead of a fever, hid in the bowels of London because the law held her to be a dangerous fugitive.

Despite her exhaustion, sleep proved elusive as worry kept her mind churning. Only when Lily's thoughts drifted to a certain, principled police officer did her tension ease and sleep claim her.

CHAPTER

9

Damp hair stuck to Lily's skin from the heat of the ovens despite the ice that threatened to trip her on the way to work this morning. The bakery had only been open since the sun came up, but she'd woken the ovens some time ago.

The bell over the doorway gave its jumble of notes, a common sound since the doors were unlocked for customers. Lily caught herself leaning toward the archway to the front, not for the first time. She straightened, taking hold of the heavy baking tray with both hands so the pastries wouldn't slip off.

Thoughts of Henry continued to plague her, and she looked forward to his daily visit with far too much joy than was proper. Daydreams even showed him helping her to protect Samantha, a sign of her foolishness more than any other. He would scorn Lily and imprison her and her sister both if ever he knew. She just wished she were strong enough to do more than lock her sister in a stable like an unwanted barn cat. With a man like Henry to speak for her, she could have gotten work on a ship to the Continent without difficulty, space for Samantha as well.

She shook her head, a sour laugh breaking free as she considered the very principles she found so compelling would lead Henry to turn her in. Life didn't offer her such chances. She'd best pay attention to the job she had rather than longing for a different future. When the Channel thawed would be soon enough to worry about how she'd manage to get them across, and then thoughts of Henry, or any form of life on this shore, would be left behind her.

The pendulum clock Mr. Cooper had on a shelf in the front struck the seventh hour, its resonant chimes putting the doorbell to shame. Unlike the doorbell, the clock did not lie, and Henry had become quite punctual, arriving smartly at seven.

Lily went to the batch of buns she'd just pulled from the oven, warm and aromatic, and started putting them into a cloth for him. She wrapped them tight so they wouldn't cool down too much before he reached the station, giving the task her full concentration.

As much as she tried not to listen, her attention had drifted to the front room where she could hear the rumble of his deep voice greeting the girls.

"So Officer Henry, I heard a funny thing the other day."

Lily recognized Jane's lilting soprano and took a step toward the front. That sound rarely boded well.

"Did you now?"

"Yes. I heard tell that you're a viscount. To think our local officer of the beat is secretly part of the nobility. What a laugh."

Lily cringed at the girl's incredulous tone, knowing no matter how ridiculous the rumor, it must strike a man's pride to hear a pretty girl so dismissive of him.

Before she could reveal herself, she caught sight of Henry's face in time to see a pained look flash across his handsome features.

"Oh, that's no rumor. It's the Queen's honest truth."

Lily froze at his words, her mind unable to absorb this truth when she'd been sure he had been courting her favor. Not that she had any plans to give in to his interest, but hadn't enough stood in the way to make anything more unnecessary?

"I am indeed a viscount."

Her mind caught up with the fact that he was still speaking in time to hear him mutter, "but it was not meant to be this way."

She remembered the flash of pain in his visage. It seemed to have deeper roots than simple pride.

"Tell me more," Jane begged. "I never imagined we had a lord in our humble shop."

Kate moved to join Jane with a rustle of fabric. Even Bettina had paused in her work of painting the loaves of bread with a wash of butter.

Lily shook off her paralysis and rushed to put an end to this badgering, Henry raising her protective instincts as he never had before.

No sooner had she stepped through the archway, though, but his smile at her arrival struck her dumb once more, her scolding left unspoken. All the troubles standing between her and this man who made her heart skip a beat washed away under the force of his attention.

Henry held her gaze for a moment longer before he turned back to the waiting girls. "My parents and older brother went down with a packet ship to the Continent last year. None survived. The title and estate then passed to me, who had never wanted it."

A gasp escaped Lily before she could school herself to silence. Title or not, they'd both recently lost parents, a bond that pulled at the ache in her heart.

Henry looked at her again with those perfect blue eyes full of honesty. "Don't distress yourself, Miss Lily. They were living their lives as they wanted. Safety is a choice not everyone is willing to make, especially when it means a reduction in opportunities. Life doesn't always work out the way it should."

When she opened her mouth to protest his dismissal, he moved his head in a gentle shake. "I'm sure my family is in a better place. Wherever they are, I doubt me they waste time regretting the life they enjoyed here. I refuse to do that service for them."

"Now no more of this sad talk," Jane said, brushing her hand on his arm in a much too forward manner, especially when she'd teased Lily about being the target of his affections often enough. Clearly his title changed things for the younger girl as well, though in the opposite fashion. "Tell us how you ended up doing a police officer's job?"

With his back turned, Lily grabbed a cloth for wiping down the counters and waved it at Jane, scowling once she caught the girl's attention. Mr. Cooper wouldn't tolerate any behavior that might undermine the reputation of his business. She only wanted to protect Jane, or so she tried to convince herself.

Henry, though, showed no offense at Jane's prying, nor did he protest her touch. He shared a smile with the lot of them, pivoting to include Lily in his audience. "I can do more good here helping people than back home lording over what is quite a small estate as estates go. Enough to keep a man, but not enough to make my absence a problem. I'd already started down this path with every expectation of my brother living to a ripe old age surrounded with children. I have people who count on me here."

"Oh, Officer Henry, we sure are grateful you decided to be here to protect us from dangers like that man yesterday," Kate broke in, equally oblivious to Lily's frantic gestures behind Henry's back.

Lily gave up on subtlety, annoyed that Kate credited Jane's rescue to Henry when Lily had been the one to pull the foolish girl out of the way. "Jane, go fetch some more buns from the back. We're fresh out here. And Kate, the oven fire needs some more coal."

Jane's pout reminded Lily of her sister, though Jane had easily ten years on Samantha. Neither dealt well in the confines of society, but only one could be imprisoned for it. Still, with the wrong customer, Jane could get herself into more trouble than she could afford.

That thought turned her attention back to Henry, who stood watching her as though he could read her mind.

"I apologize, Officer Henry," Lily said, her tone stiff and formal. "For the girls, I mean."

A strand of hair came loose from her mob cap and she brushed it off her face, losing some of her stiffness. "I don't know what's gotten into them. Your business is your own, especially what you choose to do with your life." She swallowed the second piece of his previously unknown station and busied her hands putting together a packet of jam pastries for him and his team.

"I thought I'd asked you to call me Henry." He leaned over the counter, coming much too close for her comfort, doubly so when he caught the errant strand and tucked it behind her ear, sending shivers down the side of her face.

Lily scrubbed her tingling cheek and gave the folds of paper around the pastries much more attention than the task required.

"I am sorry as well," he said, half under his breath, though for what she couldn't tell. "It seems I owe you an apology of my own," Henry added, loud enough to attract the attention of Bettina and of Kate who returned from the kitchen. "I did not mean to cause such a disruption in your morning."

Flustered, Lily thrust the packet toward him. "There's no need. You were only trying to help as you always do, even when the help is to answer impertinent questions. We've kept you long enough. You can settle the account when you're in tomorrow."

Lily strangled on the last of her words as she realized she'd all but told him how she'd been paying attention to his movements.

Henry took the package from her only to set it back on the counter. "This morning has not gone as I had hoped," he said, the words low enough she decided she could ignore them, at least until he caught her hand and forced her to look at him.

"Miss Lily, I find you compelling. Your look is fine, but it's how you care for those around you, how you put so much of yourself into your work, that has won me over. Surely you've noticed."

He waited, but Lily could think of no words at all, her mind a blank page.

Henry coughed something that sounded awfully like a smothered laugh before he shook his head. "I suspect this morning's revelations have offered some confusion, but my intentions have not changed."

"And what intentions are those." Bettina came to stand behind Lily, putting a hand on her shoulder.

Henry nodded at the older woman. "I wish to invite Miss Lily for a stroll through the flower market. " He turned back to Lily before she could figure out a response. "Would you agree to come with me on your next day off? The pickings are slim as they come only from conservatories, but I've heard they are still quite lovely, especially with the days turning so grim."

"Say you'll go," Jane called in a loud whisper. "If you don't, I'll have him take me along."

Lily shook her head at the other girl, but Henry only laughed.

"Say you'll go," he mimicked Jane and gave her such a wistful look that she'd nodded in agreement before she could think of all the reasons it was a bad idea.

"Splendid." Henry gave her a cheeky grin, swept the package off the counter, and turned for the door.

Having so far failed to keep separate from this enticing man, Lily gave herself permission to admire the fine cut of his uniform and how well he filled it for she couldn't sink much further, a luxury she regretted when he spun at the door.

Lily grabbed for the towel and pretended she'd been focused on cleaning the crumbs from the counter, though she doubted she'd fooled anyone.

Henry lifted the flat package and gave a rueful headshake. "I'd get nothing but ribbing if I were to return to the station with these. The first time was lesson enough. They prefer something a bit more hearty."

She took the packet from his hand, blushing as she realized what she'd done in her desperation to appear busy. Jam pastries were expensive and kept on hand only for the wealthiest of customers this late in the year.

"The men look for your fresh-from-the-oven buns each day to warm themselves inside and out," he offered as though to ease her embarrassment. "I'll keep the pastries for my staff, but don't want to disappoint."

Lily blushed even harder, grateful only for knowing he had enough to afford the pastries where others might not. "You do not have to take them. The mistake was mine. I'm sure your staff can make you whatever pastries you desire." She shifted the package further from him.

Henry caught her hand for the second time, gently tugging the packet from beneath her fingers. "If Bessie hears I turned aside jam pastries from Cooper's when I had them in my hand, she'll leave the meat out of my supper. You wouldn't want me to go hungry, now would you?"

Jane appeared then with the buns Lily had already set aside, the cloth surrounding them gently toasted by the oven's warmth.

Grateful for the interruption, Lily handed the proper package to Henry without making further mention of the pastries. "You'd best be getting on. Your fellows are most likely peckish."

He winked at Lily. "Trying hard to get rid of me, are you?"

She chose not to respond when she couldn't decide whether to protest or agree.

Henry headed out of the shop once more, glancing back when he reached the doorway, but Lily pretended not to notice as she rearranged the remaining pastries so the tray didn't look so empty. She'd already made enough of a fool of herself, and with the day barely begun.

Still, the thought of walking through glass-enclosed hot houses she'd only heard of from the customers, and with Henry at her side, brought a smile to her lips more than once throughout the rest of the day.

THE STATION bustled with activity by the time Henry arrived, teams passing information as the night shift went off in favor of the day. Henry wove through the crowded space to where his team gathered, making sure they got the pick of what he'd purchased before letting the others gobble down the rest.

"You sure are late this morning, Sergeant," Peter said as Henry reached their table. "Did you stop to scold some wrongdoer?" He made as though to peer around Henry, looking for someone being hauled to justice.

Henry dropped the two packages onto the table, the cloth for the buns falling open enough to release a hint of their aroma. "No wrongdoer this morning."

Fitz moved forward to grab a still-warm bun. "At least your dawdling didn't let all the heat out."

"She wraps them up tight, doesn't she?"

The others leaned in close at Parson's comment, unaware of the reason Henry had sought out Cooper's Bakery every morning for the past two weeks until this moment.

Henry shrugged, but memory of how she'd agreed to step out with him brought just the hint of a smile to his lips.

Ken snaked a long arm into the package then paused before withdrawing it. "I don't know why I didn't see the truth before. You like us well enough, and you have the funds, but I've wondered what we'd done to deserve such as this."

"Nothing," Jim said as though pouncing on the word. "So tell us of this pretty girl you're sniffing around. You know all about our love lives and have yet to breathe a word of yours."

"That's because he never had anything to tell." In any other team, Peter's words might have provoked a rebuke. Henry preferred the open camaraderie, or at least he normally did.

"And he's not the type to make one up like you are," Fitz inserted, coming to Henry's defense. "Leave the man in peace. Elsewise, he might just decide we're no longer deserving. Or maybe he'll keep the second package for some other team."

Before Henry could hold it back, Fitz picked up the paper and began to pull the folds open.

"That's not for you lot. Not after how you greeted my first attempt to favor you."

Despite Henry's protest, Fitz only moved faster, curiosity making his features tighten. "Jam tarts. And this deep in the season. They're a rich man's treat."

"Good thing we have a rich man before us."

Though Jim spoke, the glance Fitz shot in Henry's direction caused more discomfort. His wealth he suffered gladly. What drove the Irishman, though, was likely of more significance.

"Give us a moment, lads." Parson waved the others off, though Fitz kept hold of the pastries and even folded the paper around them once again.

"Don't worry," Henry said, attempting to lighten the suddenly tense atmosphere. "I understood you clear enough the first time, though you ate every one of them and the crumbs as well. The tarts are for my townhouse staff, not the likes of you."

Fitz came close and pressed Henry's shoulder until he sank to the bench. Parson and Fitz both crowded around him then.

"I can't say I like the smile on your lips," Parson said. "And I don't imagine Fitz does either. Them Cooper's girls have always been held to a higher standard than most, and from what I've heard, are polite and kindly, especially if you've set your eye on the one I think you have. You're a good man, and you have some pretty ideas for one of your class, but you don't think like one of us. Sometimes that works in our favor, like the notebooks, but not in this case."

Fitz broke in, "A hint of wrongdoing, and you could cost that girl everything."

"Lily—"

"I suspected so." Fitz interrupted. "My landlady is a customer. She says Lily's had it rough. Word is she just lost her father, and that after both her mother and sister passed on years earlier. You've had some losses, but not like these, Henry. She's all alone in the world. Mr. Cooper's patronage is all that keeps her out of the street."

Henry looked from one to the other, heat gathering under his collar. These were his men. He trusted them with his life, and they him. From the sound of it, they didn't even know the girl. They should be worried Lily sought to take advantage of him, not the other way round.

The thought of Lily scheming for his wealth or title brought his anger up short. His lips curved in another smile, and he shook his head. "You're right to defend her, but I'm not some randy nobleman seeking to slate my hungers without consequence."

Parson grunted. "We know you don't mean to a' purpose. It's just you live in different worlds. What might seem harmless to you could cause her the greatest of harm."

Fitz crossed both arms on his chest and simply stared.

Though Henry wanted to reassure them, he had only to remember his own questions the other night to know he had no answers. "I don't know what will come of this," he said at last. "But I have no plans to compromise her. I just want to get to know her, to understand why she draws me so. Then I'll have a better idea of what I mean to do about it."

The solemn expression on Fitz's face cracked into a laugh. "Listen to the man. He's smitten and doesn't know it yet. There's no end to this beyond a walk to the house of a real priest, not just the son of one like you, Parson. Sergeant, you need to count your bachelor days as coming to a close and start planning how to tell her the truth about who you are."

Parson straightened. "You haven't told her?"

Though the telling happened without his choice or plan, Henry allowed a moment of relief that he could give the affirmative. "Just this morning." He held up a hand to stop Parson so he could add, "Before she agreed to go walking with me."

Parson gave a stiff nod. "That's good then. But while you're figuring out your intentions, make sure to keep her situation in mind. Should you decide she's not ladylike enough to exchange rings, she needs to be able to keep a roof over her head and food on her table."

Henry didn't know what to say to the two of them, who despite Fitz laughing, still hovered close with expressions nearer to glowers than humor.

After a moment, Fitz stepped back. "Time to see if there's a bun or two left before we head out."

They walked away together, leaving Henry to consider their words. He had the strong feeling he'd suffer for it if he did Lily wrong. Good thing he had no intention of doing that whatever else he might still be figuring out.

When Lily stepped out of the bakery after the girls had left that night and firmly locked the door, she glanced around in the hopes of catching sight of Henry despite herself. No matter the inward scolding, the danger to herself and her sister, she'd agreed to step out with him. Her wayward heart refused to listen to her head where the officer was concerned.

The man sure gave her eyes something pleasant to admire, and she could find no fault either with his honesty or the way he chose to devote his life to helping people. While he had not spread word of his title, he didn't hesitate to answer the question when asked. To give up a lordship, no matter how small he made it sound, in favor of tromping the slushy streets on the lookout for miscreants spoke well for him. Any girl, any lady, even, would be honored to have him come courting.

She pulled her cloak tight around her shoulders, the falling snow dancing in the gas light's illumination. If only he didn't hold the law so highly, though she'd have little respect for him if he didn't. Her feet crunched on the already built-up layer, the chill seeping through her thin-soled boots. Like the weather, rules troubled the good and bad alike, little caring what reasons might put them under its weight.

Even had Henry not been an officer of the law, though, she couldn't waste her time on daydreams of finding the perfect companion as her father had. She had no parents to speak out for her, but more, she had Samantha. Why would a good man like Henry, or any other, sidestep all the eager young women in London in favor of taking on her dangers?

Lily's mouth quirked on one side, not enough to expose her teeth to the biting night. Should fate send such a man to her side, one willing to join his life to hers, to shoulder her burdens along with his own, it would never be someone like Henry. Never someone so tied to the law. So why did her heart keep looking in his direction?

Hiding her sister broke every rule in the judges' tomes, for all that those laws were wrong. If she were found out, that would be it for both her and Samantha. How much worse would the burden fall on an officer, a nobleman as well?

Her foolish heart ignored the reasoning in favor of tossing up images of how Henry's eyes had focused on her so intently this very morning, of the slight smile that dented the left side of his cheek. Her fingers tingled at the thought of him, and how he'd gained her agreement before she could restrain her tongue. He hadn't even been angry at her giving him the most expensive pastries in the whole bakery. Worse, he'd teased her for it.

If, perhaps, she could hold firm against his soft wit and honest caring about those around him, there might be some purpose in this attraction after all. She could learn how long Samantha would be safe at the stables. He might just tell her about his investigations, or if she listened to his frustrations with new mechanicals spreading through London, she would know where the dangers lie.

She paused just inside the stable's side entrance to shake the snow from her shoulders, grateful only that the snow hadn't collected in the alley itself to reveal her footsteps.

Even if he were willing to share the knowledge, she'd be more likely to slip up herself as she had in accepting his invitation. Samantha's safety had to come first. If times were different, if Naturals weren't outlawed, then maybe…but she might as well wish the sky turned green and four moons rose to light her way.

The warmth from the enhanced stove seeped into her bones and drove away her worries for the moment at least. As much as she would have preferred Samantha had left well enough alone, the welcome heat comforted her.

Then all the comfort drained away, leaving Lily to shiver but not with cold.

She'd been within the stable for a good while, as her sister calculated time at least, and Samantha had neither called out nor arrived on some new transport device. The chances that Sam had finally learned to wait for Lily to announce herself measured less than none.

The folded cloth holding their dinner hit the floor as it slipped from Lily's numb hands. She raced for the tack room in the tenuous hope her sister had fallen asleep back there so didn't notice her arrival.

The sound of her sister's laugh froze Lily with a hand outstretched to shove the door wide.

There had been a time when Samantha's joy would have brought an answering smile to Lily's face, but now she had to force herself to take the last step. She concentrated on pushing the door open slow and quiet so as not to disturb the scene inside.

Whatever she found could not bode well for their safety or this meager life they'd claimed. Where would she find a better place to hide her sister?

Samantha sat on the floor in the middle of the room, her cheeks red with delight and her hands raised as though ready to clap.

Lily pushed the door open a little further to reveal the source of Samantha's amusement.

A mechanical man, no higher than a rabbit, danced for her sister. Its little arms and legs, constructed of gears and rods, spun about in a vigorous Irish jig, or what would have been vigorous had the creature been alive.

The door hit the wall before Lily even realized she'd shoved it out of her way. She ran forward and snatched up the mechanical, the way its limbs kept twitching against her palm making her skin crawl. "Sam, where did this come from? Why did you leave the barn? Whose device did you steal? You promised." Her voice rose with each question until the last words came out as a wail. Lily struggled to control the erratic beating of her heart.

As a counterpoint to her efforts, the little man twitched again. She flung it to the floor and raised a boot, intending to crush it. "Lily, don't."

Sam was on her feet, rushing over to the object before Lily could apologize for mistreating it in her instinctive revulsion at this thing that moved with no visible source of energy.

Her sister snatched up the mechanical man and held him against her chest, feet braced as though expecting a fight. "It's not what you think. I didn't break my promise. I didn't go out. The dancing man came to me."

Lily's legs went out from under her, and she landed in a cloud of dust. "You said you told them all to go away. That the mechanicals wouldn't come here."

Samantha lowered her gaze at that, staring at the toe she ground into the dirt, her feet bare now that the stove made shoes unnecessary for warmth. "He slipped in through one of the broken boards. No one saw him. I couldn't send him away. He was damaged. Hurt."

The dirt under Samantha's toe suddenly took on shapes that didn't belong as Lily realized her sister was nudging gears and other metal pieces strewn around the floor.

"You have to put it back, Sam, back into whatever it was when it came to you. You have to send the mechanical on its way before someone comes looking. Bad enough mechanical devices seek you out. If people see little men walking around here, just how long do you think we'll be able to keep this secret? Only Naturals can imbue objects with this semblance of life."

Samantha might have seemed older sometimes, but she was just a little girl. She wore emotions on her expressive features for all to see if any were there to look. She lacked the social experience to manage a lie even if it meant her life.

Lily rose to retrieve their dinner from the entrance. Her feet dragged as she walked, but at least Samantha had not been discovered yet. With that thing about, though, it was only a matter of time.

With the inner door left open, she could hear Samantha singing to the mechanical, that object the closest thing she'd had to a real playmate since her abilities first manifested. Lily had always been more of a mother than a friend.

Her hands shook as she picked up a hardened roll that had escaped her cloth. She couldn't help thinking of how bitterly she'd failed her mother in taking over the task of raising Sam. But Mother could not have imagined what she was asking Lily in the deathbed request. First Samantha developed a knack for mechanical objects, then their father's accident. It had taken all of Lily's strength to determine what to do next.

Running off to the Continent with little more than the clothes on their back seemed much too dangerous compared to waiting for the estate to settle. She'd never considered a future in which, rather than receiving enough to secure a ship cabin where she could hide her sister, they'd be left with nothing.

Samantha would have been so much happier there in a safe haven even if they had to beg in the streets to make their way once they'd left the ship rather than hiding here in the country of their birth. She would have had more company, and the company of those who understood her as Lily would never be able to. If only Lily could have seen that then.

Maybe that was why the mechanicals found their way to the stable doors. Maybe they could sense how lonely Samantha was.

Lily forced a smile on her lips as she returned to the tack room in the hopes of finding a pair of walking boots or maybe a small push wagon for carrying a lady's packages where the mechanical man had stood.

She could have wept at the sight that met her gaze when she stepped within the tack room.

The gears had been gathered up and added to the mechanical man so he stood a little taller but she could detect no significant difference in the structure.

"Samantha."

Her sister glanced up, all innocent of expression. "I know you said to return him to his original state, but you didn't want me to remake him broken. That would be cruel."

For a second time in one evening, Lily felt the need to slump to the floor, but she locked her knees and stayed upright. "What do you mean?" Her sister might be incapable of a lie, but how could she mean what she seemed to say?

Once again Samantha moved between Lily and the object. "He was a mechanical man when he came to the stables."

Lily shook her head, trying to deny what her sister said. "How can that be? No, it's of no matter. He was something before."

Samantha crossed her arms and her eyes narrowed. "You didn't say to return to his first state, Lily. I did as you asked. I remade him as he came to me, repaired, but the same form. You can't have meant to strip him of arms and legs, to trap him in an unnatural state. I cannot do something so dark-hearted, and I can't imagine you mean me to. He's been a mechanical man for oh so long. He hardly remembers what he was before."

Lily staggered over to the table to sink onto the nearest chair. "There is nothing natural about this form. It's not a 'him.' It's a collection of parts motivated by who knows what strangeness."

Though the words matched their conversation, she did not mean them for her sister. If the mechanical man had come to Samantha in this form, it meant a wild Natural had come to their section of town as well, and one with not enough sense to keep those impulses under control as Sam had to.

"It can't be that bad, Lily. Don't worry so. I made it all right. I've fixed the little man."

A strangled laugh burst from Lily as she raised her head to stare at Samantha's earnest expression. Her sister either had not heard what she said, or chose not to argue.

"You don't understand, Sam. You don't understand what this means. A Natural made that thing." She jerked her chin toward where the mechanical man stood. "A Natural who will bring the law down on our heads. Our safety depends on being quiet little mice in the pantry. He's leaving droppings in the flour so they know to set the cats on all of us." And Henry would be the one to lead the parade.

Samantha turned a frown on the mechanical, as though it, not its maker, were the cause of all their problems.

Lily didn't know whether to find relief in Samantha's understanding now when it came too late to protect them.

Then her sister's expression changed.

"No, Lily, it's you who cannot see. There's no more droppings to find. The mechanical man was broken. He was hurting. If he had a Natural, the pull to fix this mechanical would have been too great. His Natural has been and gone."

It was Lily's turn to stare at the little man. Maybe Sam's loneliness had less of a draw than whatever motivated this object.

Samantha might be imagining a person just passing through, but Lily knew well enough from watching her sister that Naturals couldn't leave their own creations behind by accident. As Sam said, the pull would have been too great.

She wrapped both arms around her middle and squeezed as though she could hold all the worry and fear inside. Henry had done this. Henry and his team.

This broken, hopeless creation existed because of the capture they'd made. A Natural had been locked away, slowly to go insane from feeling the pull and yet never able to act on it. Henry was responsible, and he would do the same to Samantha if they were discovered.

Despite the risk, though, she couldn't deny her sister. She'd locked Samantha up here all alone for several months, visiting as much as she could, but it was no life for a young girl. Yet it was the only life she could offer Samantha that would keep her safe.

"Make sure the mechanical man stays in the stable. It must never be seen by anyone."

Samantha's squeal of delight was enough of a reward, though it carried with it a fierce twist of guilt.

Lily experienced a restless night, haunted by the joy in Samantha's face as she bonded with the mechanical man, or whatever it was Naturals did to connect to their creations. Both seemed happier for the claiming. This could have been Sam's life already, and not one damaged mechanical seeking out any Natural, but creations of her own.

She swore, not for the first time, she'd give Samantha that gift. She'd find a way across the Channel and find one of the safe havens on the Continent even if it meant leaving her sister there because Lily would not be allowed to stay. Even without the fugitive laws, she would never find someone who didn't look on a Natural with hate and fear. She would not torment her sister by surrounding Sam with such in her own home. Better the isolation of a stable than never knowing when Lily's husband would decide the risk too great and turn Sam in.

The low rumble of voices brought Lily's head up as she walked toward the stable to check on Samantha before continuing on to the bakery, something she shouldn't make a habit of in the morning, but with the mechanical man's arrival, she needed the reassurance. This early, there were rarely other pedestrians, and those tended to lean into the chill wind and march silently onward, at least in winter. The weather matched her dim mood.

Her gaze skipped over a darkness where there was already shadow, and then came back to recognize a familiar dark blue coat in one of the doorways.

Her heart leapt at the sight of Henry, only to sink when she realized what it meant for him to be here, so close to the stable. Someone must have reported the mechanical man.

This had been why she'd balked at the thought of courtship between them, why she should never have accepted his invitation. And yet, now she had no choice but to use their connection to distract him from his task, one more choice he'd condemn her for should he discover the truth.

Her chest ached, as much from hating the betrayal as from fear.

He had done her no harm. If anything, he'd been good to her, and his interest in another time would have been quite welcome. She now returned his regard with a knife in the back, not just for his person, but also for his profession.

Her steps dragged as she made her reluctant way over to him.

She stepped off the curb on her side to cross at the same moment he turned from the doorway where he must have been interviewing the occupant. Her gaze brushed an unfamiliar face above the familiar uniform, and some of her tension eased. She should have noticed how this man's shoulders were broader, how his legs lacked the elegant curves she'd observed on Henry's fit form. This section had never been part of his patrol as far as she knew.

"Miss? A word, if you please? Do you come from nearby?"

Stillness entered Lily's mind and soul as though the world froze in that moment. She hadn't figured out what to tell Henry to persuade him, but in her relief at discovering a stranger, she'd failed to realize any hold she might have had was lost. Her thoughts spun in circles, one overarching command clear.

He must not connect the mechanical man with the abandoned stables one street over. And he must not connect Lily with the stables either.

The last finally gave her troubled mind a direction, and she drew in a breath of frost-laden air. "No, Sir. I live down there a ways. I'm off to work now."

She hadn't intended to mimic her landlady's accent, but a hint of it sounded in her words, another source of confusion should this man mention their encounter to Henry.

"You come this way often?"

Lily nodded, having no choice when any other explanation would involve too convoluted a lie.

The officer bent to hold his hand at knee level. "You seen a mechanical man about so high?"

Relief almost brought an unfortunate laugh from her lips as she answered honestly. "I have not." Even with Samantha's modifications to restore the mechanical man, it had been half the height indicated.

The man sighed heavy enough to ruffle his thick mustache. "It's too early in the morning to be chasing whiskey dreams brought on by tales of that Natural they captured," he muttered. He glanced up as if startled to see her still standing there. "Well then, be on your way now, Miss. Don't you be worrying about things down here. We'll get it all sorted."

Lily didn't wait to be told twice. There was no way she could sneak off to see her sister now. She had to continue on to work or chance drawing his suspicion. Her feet knew the path well enough, having trod it for many months now since they'd had to vacate their childhood home. Lily focused her attention on prayer instead. If only Samantha would be smart and quiet. If only the mechanical man, who brought so much joy and had no other place to go, wouldn't make a noise and reveal her sister.

If only they'd both still be hidden and safe when she got off that evening. Lily pleaded with fate to grant her this much at least.

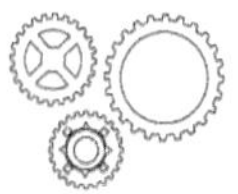

"OH, LILY..."

Caught in the act of inserting a new tray of muffins into the oven, Lily sent the tray home and levered the door closed before coming out to the front to see why Jane had called for her.

Kate and Jane started giggling as soon as they saw her.

"Your beau is coming. We know how disappointed you were when he didn't show up this morning." Kate pressed both hands to the sides of her face, dragging her cheeks down, but the girl had no idea what had driven Lily's concern when the hour chimed and Henry had not appeared.

She turned to glance out the door as Bettina held it open for a customer whose hands were full of fresh bread.

Sure enough, Henry could be seen approaching the bakery on the far side of the street with his usual purposeful stride. Nothing about him indicated he came on official business this time, but his absence made her fear they'd discovered Sam, and rather than finding his late arrival reassuring, she worried something else brought him to her door.

His gaze tangled with hers, and an enticing smile put a dimple in his cheek as he noticed her watching.

The tension drained from Lily, and her heart quickened at sharing even so small a moment of connection.

Henry stepped off the curb, still holding her attention.

A steam-powered cart rumbled past him, faster than any such vehicle should have been able to move. It brushed close enough that Henry had to jerk back to avoid being hit.

Lily almost missed the driver's shouted apology over the thundering of her heart, but it didn't seem to soften Henry's expression as he stared at the cart, clearly choosing between an undignified run after the disappearing vehicle on icy roads and letting the man go without a rebuke.

Though he turned back to face the shop, Lily had seen enough to remind her why she had no business developing an attachment to this man. He might have chosen her in this moment, but he'd been torn. If he'd had any chance of catching the lawbreaker, his feet would be pounding after the man as she watched.

Lily searched the nearest racks and seized an almost empty tray to carry into the back, desperate to escape before he came in. She could not face him, not on this day when every time she looked at him she'd wonder if he'd be the one to take her to prison.

From the front came enthusiastic greetings, the girls not deterred by her absence in the slightest. "Oh, won't you hang on for a little? I'm sure Lily will be right out," Kate said, loud enough to make it clear she meant Lily to hear.

His voice rumbled in reply, the tones too deep carry.

Jane laughed, and Lily imagined the girl's hand brushing Henry's coat sleeve, Jane as quick to ignore the proprieties as Henry had been with Lily. "It's not the sight of you she's running from but the secret she holds in her own breast. That's why she finds excuses to hide from you, Officer Henry. You need only tease it out of her."

Lily's hand slipped.

The tray she'd been holding crashed against the shelf, only luck making it an empty one.

Bettina rushed in to check on her, the noise too loud not to reach the front even as it masked the conversation she'd been straining to overhear.

"Are you all right?"

Lily pushed back her escaping hair and sighed. "I'm fine, Bettina. I didn't drop the tray fully, and it had nothing on it to go to waste."

The older woman shook her head and pressed a hand to Lily's arm. "That's not what I meant, and you know it. You've been jumpy all day, and now you're hiding from Officer Henry? You know that young man comes here more for a moment of your company than the baked goods he buys."

Lily managed a laugh. "You know who and what he is. It's a harmless flirt. That's all one of his station would want with a shop girl."

"Believe what you will. I've seen how his gaze follows you. That man has fixed his attention firmly, and why else would you have agreed to go walking with him?"

Sighing, Lily shifted some rolls to the tray she'd brought into the back. "I should never have agreed. It was a weak moment. If I could figure out a way, I'd cry off now, with two days still to go before I've a day off."

Bettina shook her head. "You shouldn't trifle with hearts like that, Lily, not his, and not your own. I've seen you look on him as well. Now give me that tray to finish. I believe you have a customer to attend to."

As much as Lily wanted to deny it, Bettina only made the same hint the girls teased about. They had no idea what the consequences would be if he cared enough to dig deeper into her life. Bettina was wrong about Henry, though. If he were so serious, he'd be asking about a parent to speak to, of which she had none.

Lily picked up a different tray that already held a full load of muffins. "I'll bring these forward."

Bettina's smile should have encouraged, but the older woman didn't understand Lily's purpose. She had no intention of hinting that she welcomed his attention, or revealing the crush Kate and Jane teased him about.

Where before she'd considered seeking information about the search for Naturals, between the mechanical man who had taken up residence in the stables and the girls implying she had some deep dark secret, it would only raise questions. Instead, she planned to show him exactly how little she shared his interest until he withdrew the invitation, thinking her more intrigued by what his wealth offered than the man himself.

"There you are, Lily," Jane cried as soon as Lily stepped free of the back. "Bettina chase you out?"

She sent both girls a quelling glance as she placed the muffins on display before turning to Henry as though just noticing him there. "Do you want your usual order for the station?" She choked back a comment on the late hour rather than indicate she was aware of his comings and goings, something unlikely to support her effort to project indifference.

He gave her an intent look before twisting to face the girls.

Lily caught the edge of his wink to the girls, then he turned back to her.

"I've come to settle the bill from yesterday, and yes, more hot buns would please the officers if you have them."

Lily fought her blush as she remembered what had kept him from paying his bill. "There's a tray just out in the back. Kate will get them for you." Her voice came out harsher than she'd hoped, but at least he couldn't question her distance.

Something changed in Henry's expression, a subtle movement she wouldn't have noticed if she hadn't been watching him all too closely. He glanced toward the door as though regretting his decision to come, a thought that both eased Lily's tension and started up a new one.

His shoulders relaxed within his thick wool coat, and he faced her with a soft smile. "I hear you make a special frosted pastry. Seeing as there are no other customers, would you have time to make me one? I deserve a treat after almost being bowled over in the street, don't you think?"

Any relief vanished as he trapped her with the request. He'd already removed the excuse of customers, and she knew the girls would be quick to eliminate any other impediment, thinking to help her. Much better that he'd taken her coldness as a rejection of his suit.

"It'll take me a moment to mix up the frosting. Aren't you due back at the station?"

"I have the time. I'm happy to wait."

He jumped in with a response before she could discourage him further. Any more attempts, and she'd be denying a customer. Lily wished she'd taught one of the others how to make the frosting and swirl it just right. Or that she'd never come up with the special treat in the first place.

Pride meant she couldn't offer him less than a perfect job. She couldn't foist the task off on any other for all that lingering in his presence made her uneasy in more ways than she wanted to consider.

Her mind only half on the task, she whipped up the frosting to its proper thickness and smoothed it onto the pastry so it formed an alien landscape, giving it an extra twist just because.

When Lily finished, she pushed the pastry toward him in the hope he'd take it and leave.

He responded with the smile that turned her insides to jelly and made her dream of things that could never be.

HENRY WATCHED Lily's cheeks turn pink when he smiled at her. He took it as proof she felt at least a little inclined toward him despite her efforts to keep their conversations to her proper tasks. She behaved as a respectable young woman should.

He leaned forward to breathe in the hearty scent of yeast and cinnamon that always seemed to linger around Lily more than any other of the girls. Though his police coat made the heat of the shop stifling, when Lily graced him with her presence, he felt more comfortable here in the overly warm bakery than anywhere else.

Lily's blush darkened, but she didn't protest his behavior. This gave the girls' hints more weight than it seemed when she'd been so cool. She was quick to put others before herself, shouldering burdens well beyond what anyone should expect of a young woman. She needed someone to think of her first, to put her wishes before those of any other.

Henry had every intention of being that person.

When he'd seen her lock up the bakery at night, she always rushed off as though to another urgent task. He'd imagined an invalid parent for her to be working so hard at such a young age, though from what Fitz and Parson said, it had to be a more distant relative. The connection he'd felt had only grown since he'd spoken to her that first time. He could understand the need to help others, and the weight life put on a person, willing or not.

His attraction had strengthened until he couldn't imagine a day going by without seeing her. He'd needed to speak with the inspector this morning, the only reason for coming in so late. Though he could have waited for the next day, her smile meant more to him than the time to come here instead of eat his midday meal.

"Your pastry, Officer Henry."

He almost laughed at the reminder, but his chest tightened at the breathless way she said the words. His gaze caressed the curve of her shoulder, the delicate line of her neck.

"Thank you, Miss Lily. It smells divine." Henry met her gaze and held it a bit longer than propriety dictated. "I look forward to our outing."

She ducked her head and turned from him, picking up the icing bag for an excuse.

"Is there a problem?"

For a heart-stopping moment, he thought she would call it off. Her expression closed in on itself, but before she could say the words, he interrupted with, "If an afternoon is too much, at least let me walk you home. You leave here so late."

Lily stared at him, eyes wide as though startled or scared.

She blinked, and he wondered if he'd imagined the moment.

"No, I've been looking forward to the flower market. I've heard of it from customers, and it sounds miraculous."

Her answer wiped away any thought that she'd attempted to turn him aside, and he gazed on her in delight, long enough that she must have wondered why he still stood there like a lovesick schoolboy.

Loose strands of blond hair lay plastered to her forehead, noth-ing like the elegant hairstyles of a lady of his class, but the way they half-obscured her eyes intrigued him. She resembled nothing less than a barn kitten peering out of a bush as it considered whether the strip of bacon in his hand could be trusted.

She brushed the hair out of her way, but the image stayed strong enough to bring a chuckle to his lips. He couldn't help teasing her as the girls had teased him. "Maybe it's time for me to dig out your secret, Lily. To bring it into the light."

Before he could say anything more, she blanched, all color draining from her expression. Her fingers tightened on the bag, and a squirt of cream icing flew across the room.

The words strangled in his throat.

"Oh dear." She stared at the mess as though she could imagine no worse a crisis. Then, she caught her skirt up with a free hand and ran for the kitchen, something he'd never thought to see her do.

How could she have been so stupid?

Lily braced herself against the racks in the far corner of the bakery. Her eyes stung with unshed tears, springing from a mix of anger and despair.

He hadn't meant anything by his question. He had only been continuing the tease from the other girls. He hadn't known there was anything to know.

But now he did.

All his senses, fine-tuned to the law, had to be set on alert by her foolish reaction. She'd managed to distract him from the idea of walking her home well enough. Everything had been fine, though her plan to have him think her cold shattered faster than a porcelain cream pitcher.

Lily buried her face in both hands, knowing she could only hide for so long, and when he saw her next, he'd have no dimpled smile. Instead, he'd bombard her with questions she could not answer no matter what the cost to herself. And yet, what would Samantha do if Henry took Lily down to the station and locked her away for good when she refused?

The scrape of a boot brought her head up. Lily stared at the unlikely sight of Henry here, in the kitchen, where he must know he had no right to be.

She shrank away, her back pressed hard enough to the racks that they creaked against her weight.

He caught her chin with the tips of his fingers, blocking any escape. "I apologize for my presumption in coming back here, but I know you."

His words made no sense.

Lily's gaze jolted to meet his. What she saw there held no accusation. Instead, his expression held worry.

Something deep inside her loosened at the sight. She'd been on her own so long, always the worrier with no one to care about what happened to her beyond the bakery girls, none of whom knew the first thing about what put the tension into her muscles.

"I've been watching you for long enough," Henry continued, "to know whatever brought the pale to your cheeks cannot be your fault. Tell me what frightens you. It's my job to help. You have to confide in me so I can do what's necessary to end your troubles."

His demand frightened her more, but then his earnest tone sank into Lily, and she didn't resist when he pulled her head down to lay against his broad chest though she knew the proprieties were far gone in this situation. Should the girls come back here on whatever errand might claim their time, manufactured or real, they would misunderstand.

Still, Lily could not summon the energy to push away from his comfort. She'd grown tired of hiding, lying, always worrying she'd make a mistake, or already had in not escaping London with her sister the moment she received word of her father's death.

"I have contacts throughout London. Whoever is making you tremble will back off when he realizes you have me to protect you. More than that, you have the force of the law on your side."

Where his physical support had comforted, this restored her tension at ten times the strength.

Lily shoved away, brushing back her loose hair to gain a moment to collect her thoughts. She had almost confessed. She had almost given up everything—and to an officer of the law—just to share the burden of her secret.

Face averted, she stepped around him to open the oven door and hide in the gust of released steam. "You are mistaken. I have no troubles to speak of. None, that is, but what my employer will think should he come to check on the bakery and find you where you have no business being. If you want to be of help to me, you'll please be on your way. Surely there are those at the station waiting on you."

"But Lily—"

"Just go." She kept her voice firm only because of all the practice doing the same for Samantha while her heart skipped off beat at some new fright. The way her first name came smooth off his tongue laid support for the girls' teasing, but whatever he offered, she had no ability, nor wish, to pursue.

HENRY STARED at Lily's back, at first unwilling to believe she'd refused his help. Despite her words, the tension rocking her form even now showed she had some trouble coming down on her head. He doubted it had anything to do with her patron, Mr. Cooper.

Still, she did not turn, choosing instead to bustle about the kitchen doing whatever tasks she could find.

He knew them to be an excuse so she wouldn't have to meet his gaze, but unlike some who joined the police force to command others, Henry didn't believe his position gave him any right to bend others to his will. As much as he wanted to grab hold of her and make Lily confront whatever scared her, using his strength would be more of the same, and the last thing he wanted was to tarnish her reputation even without Parson and Fitz checking on his behavior.

Mr. Cooper had not been present any of the times Henry had come to the bakery, or when he had passed it in the commission of his duties of late. He doubted the man would choose this moment to show, but he'd seen himself how quick the girls were to gossip, as they most likely were this very moment. She did not deserve their prying any more than to have him put her nature into question.

He could linger here no longer and must leave with his questions unanswered for the time being.

Henry snapped his heels together and gave her a salute she didn't turn to see. "I'll bother you no further then, Miss Lily. Please accept my apologies for the intrusion." Unlike before, he strengthened his tones so they would carry to the front in the hopes of curbing tongues. He no more meant the apology than he intended to let this matter fade. Henry planned to help her whether she will it or not.

When he stepped beyond the shelter of the back kitchen, three pairs of eyes were caught staring. The girls turned away to pretend focus on whatever tasks they found to do, but from the splashes of red on each visible cheek, they knew he'd seen. Henry could only hope the embarrassment would keep them from spreading tales with little grounding in truth.

"Miss Bettina, if you would please take my payment?"

The gray-haired matron rubbed her hands down the starched apron she wore wrapped around her waist and came to count out his coins.

"It's payment for the two days of buns, six jam pastries, and this one," he said as she stumbled over the amount. Then he realized she might not have enough learning to do her ciphers, another way Lily stood out among the rest. "I counted it proper." He would not get Lily in trouble for this either.

"That's all fine then, Officer Henry. If you can't be trusted to make this good, who can?"

He wished Lily felt the same, at least about trusting him to make her troubles go away.

With a touch to his hat as acknowledgement and a smile for all three girls, he picked up the two packets and made his exit. Henry may have overstepped his bounds as both a customer of the bakery and a potential suitor for Lily's hand, but he would find a way to make it up to Lily. She'd shown her own inclination in that moment of weakness when she sank against him, and again when she spoke of looking forward to their outing.

If this trouble was what kept them apart, what made her pull away, rather than the ailing relative he'd first supposed, she need not have tried to protect him. He fancied himself well capable of handling what came his way. And more, he had resources she might not have considered when she rejected his comfort. Perhaps she thought his interference would make the situation worse, or that he'd turn from her if he discovered the truth of it, but she had wound her way around his heart almost without him noticing.

She didn't understand the same tenacity that made him a good officer would keep him from walking away. Now that he knew someone he cared for needed his help, nothing could dissuade him.

Despite what she'd said, Lily clearly had some kind of trouble hanging over her, a trouble so deep she feared to ask for assistance. This meant he had even more reason to ignore her wishes and get to the bottom of this. No young woman on his patrol should fear the coming day.

His strides ate up the distance between the bakery and the station as he contemplated his next act. He might not believe in abusing his position, but he could not see how anyone who troubled an upright young woman like Lily could be on the proper side of the law. He had only to figure out what was going on, and he could solve this problem for her once and for all.

If she didn't trust him enough to tell him herself then he'd just have to find out by other means.

A smile creased his face and Henry developed a bounce to his step as he finished his journey in a much better humor than he'd begun it.

Lily felt so unsettled by the events of the day that she almost accepted Bettina's offer to stay in her place and close the bakery. Only the awareness that nothing remained to be done, a fact Bettina could hardly fail to notice, and her need to go see Samantha on today of all days, held her back. She'd broken the rules, both of the bakery and of her life, in letting Henry too close, entertaining, even for a heartbeat, the idea that she could have a love in her life beyond her sister.

The normal existence she'd carved out of her unusual circumstances now seemed so distant between Henry and the mechanical man finding Samantha. She could hardly fathom that she'd be able to keep Sam secret long enough for the ice to break so they could make their way to the Continent and true safety.

That dark thought kept her company while she waited out the girls until such time as she could leave without anyone tracking her movements. The sky had darkened beyond the door, and gusts of snowflakes warned her the outside would seep any warmth from her skin and even her bones. Still, she grabbed the last cloak from the stand without hesitation.

Considering how restless her sister had been of late, if Lily arrived much past when she normally did, maybe Samantha would wander outside to find her. And as close a connection as she'd made to the mechanical man, that dratted creature would most likely trail behind Samantha as well.

Lily pulled the cloak about her as she sent a final glance over the bakery.

If only she could bring Samantha here. Mr. Cooper's belief in the traditional ways over newfangled mechanical aids meant little to trigger her sister's bouts, but to show up with a child would raise the kinds of questions a woman of her situation could not afford even without her sister's special nature.

A vision of the bakery transformed by her sister much as Samantha had improved first the stove and then the mechanical man drifted through her mind. The girls would never have to worry about losing some pay when the stove heated unevenly. The trays might not slip off the rack and send their contents tumbling to the floor. Perhaps a little mechanical man could stand sentinel against the rodents who attempted to get into the bakery stores.

Dreams of a world where Naturals worked alongside others toward a common goal vanished as Lily stepped beyond the bakery's warmth into the frigid outdoors.

The wind fought for control of the door, but after a struggle, Lily managed to pull it shut. Her fingers grew chilled to the bone as she turned the metal key to secure the building. She tucked both hands deep into her cloak, clutching her dinner packet under its woolen folds.

The fight with the door and controlling her unruly cloak took all her focus at first, but a deeper chill caught Lily as she started down the street as though she were prey to some stalking predator.

She let go of one edge of cloth and used its wild flapping as an excuse to turn, but though she checked both sides of the street, no one seemed to be paying particular attention to her.

Like Lily, the few visible people were all bundled up, crouching against the wind and snow, their heads down and feet moving steadily on the path home.

Movement caught her eye, but when she looked a second time, she saw only shadow filling the recessed doorway of a shop on the other side. No sign of a person lurking. The owner or his employees had left an awning unfurled above the door despite the wind. The gaily-colored cloth snapped and fluttered, threatening to tear free of its binding. She doubted it would still be attached to its iron frame come morning. Its frantic lashing must have been what caught her eye.

She turned back, both edges of her cloak caught firmly in her fingers to prevent the chill wind from sneaking inside.

No one had been watching her. One careworn woman, in a town filled with those whose purses held more coin and whose faces held fewer worries, attracted little attention.

What hung over her shoulder had less to do with another person than what she'd risked so few hours before. She'd come so close to failing her sister in the worst way, to revealing Samantha in a moment of weakness when police already searched the area, and to one who held the title of officer.

Lily could not afford to be weak. More than just her dignity rested on that truth. Samantha's very life, and quite possibly Lily's own, were at risk.

Her guilty conscience rode her back on this dark night, driven both by memory of what she'd almost done and the realization of just how fragile her hold on their secret had become.

It took all of Henry's will not to step out of the sheltering alcove to offer her a hand when he saw Lily struggling with the door. Then he thought she'd caught sight of him regardless, but though she stared right at him, the mad flapping of the awning above seemed to reassure her. Or rather, it sent her on her way.

He wanted to ease the burdens that curved her shoulders more than he'd ever wanted anything, but to do so, he needed to work without her knowledge. The young woman had a strong core, and a sense of pride and independence rarely seen in man or woman. She would not accept his help willingly, something she'd made clear that very day, but he would not accept her refusal either.

Snow flurries slapped his face as he moved from the doorway to follow Lily. She'd gone far enough that she wouldn't notice him, though he kept a careful watch on her back, ready to pretend a different direction should she turn.

Wrapped up tight in his dark coat, she'd be unlikely to recognize him. The wind and snow offered that much in return for the chill, and this late at night, the gas lamps weren't strong enough to combat the weather and reveal him.

As street corner after street corner passed, Henry wondered just how much further Lily had to go before she came to a place where she could rest her head. He'd stood outside the bakery for some time, watching the last of the customers and finally the other girls leave before Lily finished her work. She labored hard during the day and deserved better than this.

Soon, though, the careful stalking brought back different memories, ones that carried a weight of grief as heavy as any burden Lily might bear.

Henry and his brother used to play this game whenever their father came to town to press a matter of concern before the House of Lords. They'd honed their tracking skills by following or attempting to lose the tail, a victory claimed by whomever caught the other, either by keeping the tail, or doubling back and turning follower into followed.

The responsibilities of adulthood put an end to their games, Robert taking up his role as heir and Henry joining the police force. He used those same skills now, never imagining the woman to claim his heart would have need of them, for all she denied him the right. He would not chance losing Lily to whatever caused her fright as he had lost both parents and brother.

His hands tightened into fists, the normally supple leather gloves stiff with cold. Henry pushed back memories that threatened to overwhelm him and glanced ahead in time to see Lily take a sudden turn into an alley that ran along the side of what looked to be an abandoned hire horse stable.

Cursing his inattention, Henry surged after her, but by the time he reached the alley, no sign of Lily remained. Even the light dusting of snow failed to hold her footsteps against the wind's onslaught. He'd lost the game, but worse, he'd lost her.

Unlike his childhood games, this loss did not mean he could expect a challenge from behind. Lily would not come after him if ever he proved unlucky enough for her to discover his pursuit. He had to save her from her troubles before she'd accept he had been right to interfere.

Henry raised his collar, more to give himself something to do than because the thick fabric no longer protected his neck. He started down the alley, but all the view offered was a hint of light at the far end, proof a street large enough for streetlamps marched on the other side. She had been too far ahead of him to remain in sight on the other end, and from there, she could have gone either direction or taken any turn.

He pivoted with parade-ground precision and stomped back the way he'd come, his prints remaining to mock him as he hit a deeper patch of snow at the alleyway mouth, sheltered from the wind.

No one had made so strong an impression on his life as Lily had since the tragedy of losing his family. She was the first to bring joy back to his heart, to make him look forward to each day. Neither his police work, nor his elevation to the peerage and its attendant rewards had softened the blow. Only Lily had that power.

He would pay better attention next time. He wouldn't lose her trail, and he would solve her troubles so he could pursue her with a clear conscience on both their parts.

There had been a time when the pressure to marry, the pressure to produce an heir, had seemed too great. When eager heiresses or daughters of peers sought his attention, he'd done everything possible to escape their grasp.

Now, despite the differences between them and the difficulties that it might pose, he had begun to consider much more than just stepping out with Lily. He could see bringing forth a new generation of Stapletons with her, ones just as determined to protect the weak and make the world a little less harsh than ever he had been. From how she treated those around her, Lily would be just as motivated by the goal to prove one person could make a difference as his family had been for generations.

"CAN'T YOU stay just a little longer? My mechanical man has another dance to show you. It'll make you laugh, I promise."

Lily shook her head, ignoring both Samantha's pleas and her own longing to lock herself away in this shelter, never again to face the dangers and complications of the world beyond that door. She pulled Samantha in for one final hug, then squeezed her sister's hand to break their last contact.

"You know I have to, Sam. I've stayed too long as it is, and my reputation will suffer even if no one discovers why I'm late." Lily couldn't have said why she expected Samantha to understand when the little girl had almost no exposure to the real world, though maybe she spoke the explanation more for herself than her sister.

Mrs. Marsh had warned her often enough, in words of praise for Mr. Cooper, to keep free of rumors or goings on that might taint her. And more than just her lodgings were at stake. Even if her landlady suspected something so mundane as a lover rather than the truth, Lily would lose the job that kept them fed and clothed as well as putting wood into the belly of Samantha's modified stove. Mr. Cooper's friendship would not hold against evidence she'd become less than respectable.

The world seemed full of traps for the unwary, traps doubly set for someone like her who had a dangerous secret.

Her first step into the chill night came as an unpleasant slap. Lily tugged her cloak as tight against her as she could. How much easier it would be to live here with Samantha instead of maintaining yet another normal front. But what would they do for money then? And how would she explain why she lived in a stable like a squatter. Even without the connection between Mr. Cooper and her landlady, such wild behavior would not pass unnoticed for long. A stranger's comment about seeing her, when added to another's and another's, would come back to those with the power to condemn her.

Lily blinked to adjust to a deeper dark than she'd expected, the sky as weighty as her thoughts. At least the snow no longer fell, and the wind had died down after pushing the unmelted flakes into drifts.

The alley's mouth beckoned, a nearby gas lamp casting its faint yellow glow into the darkness and reflecting off the mound of snow that had gathered where the streets crossed. As she neared, Lily could see footprints and tracks from the occasional steam cart marring the fallen snow around the lamppost, a further sign life went on about her, unaware of just what she harbored nearby. If any who'd made those tracks came to discover a Natural sheltered in the old stable, genteel men and women would be likely to take up fire and sticks to remove the menace of an eight-year-old girl with a knack for improving mechanisms.

Lost in thought, Lily stumbled as her boot sank into the deeper snow at the end of the alley. Her bare hands disappeared beneath the cold white fluff, sending a shiver down her spine.

She braced already chilled fingers to push back upright when her gaze fell on the space between her hands.

Lily stared, the cold forgotten.

A heavy boot print dented the snow, deep enough that the man—or the size spoke of no one but—must have stood watching for a while.

She jerked to her knees and glanced back the way she'd come, in the direction the boot print pointed. The alley's steep walls kept all but a light dusting of snow from collecting there, her recent steps barely discernible. If the watcher had gone to the stable door, or moved past it on the way to other places, she would never know. It seemed her sense of being followed might not have been solely triggered by her guilty conscience though.

Lily rose the rest of the way only to notice another print, this one turned back toward the street. This had not been a coincidence. A man had watched the alley for some time before continuing on to wherever he had been headed.

A chill that had little to do with the cold lay claim to her, and she pulled her cloak even tighter.

The only comfort lay in that if there had been someone watching her as it seemed, he'd left unsatisfied.

She'd spent long enough with her sister for there to be a mob gathered here, or for the police to have come. Instead, she found nothing but a boot print. She would have to be satisfied by that sign that they'd escaped notice, as much as fear threatened to paralyze her.

Straightening her shoulders with effort, Lily started off toward her home. It seemed they had not been discovered that night, though it had been close. Still, the need to be seen at her lodgings had not changed.

Lily would have to take better care, to vary her path. Falling into habits made things all too easy for those intent on squirreling out her secrets.

CHAPTER 15

Memory of those heavy footprints still haunted her as the morning dawned with unseasonable warmth, a reminder of the spring yet to come.

"You think too hard," Bettina said, laying a hand on Lily's shoulder.

Lily tried to hide her jump as though she were moving toward the back.

"You should get out and enjoy the sunshine. I hardly needed my scarf this morning to keep the cold from slipping under my cloak. It won't last, you know. Already the wind is picking up, and tomorrow it could snow again."

Lily pushed away her worries and smiled at the older woman. "It does seem nice. The winter came on so quickly."

"All the more reason to go out there and enjoy the weather while it lasts. A young girl like you should be taking strolls in the park with a handsome fellow, not working your fingers to the bone here. Don't you have an engagement with Officer Henry?"

Lily relaxed enough to give a single laugh as she turned to straighten the muffins. "Tomorrow." Though maybe now he'd cry off.

As much as she knew that would be better for all of them, a small part of her hoped he would not. With the added fear of a stalker, having an officer around might not be the worst thing, though from the way he made her heart stumble, safety had little to do with why she looked forward to his company.

"Would that your smile were meant for me."

Lily glanced up to see the object of her thoughts standing right before her. The clock had struck the seventh hour without her noticing. "How do you know it is not?" she said without thinking, without remembering just how things ended between them the previous day until too late.

A stillness took over Henry's form, though his own smile didn't falter. "I can only dream," came his late response, along with a gaze so intent, Lily felt the blush rising to heat her cheeks.

Just then, a number of customers swept into the bakery, crowding its front room and giving Lily the excuse she needed to break their connection, "I'll collect your buns."

He caught her arm before she could flee for the back. "Address your customers' needs. I can wait."

She didn't know whether to be grateful or confused at the way he did not consider himself one of the customers. And the thought of him standing there watching her only made her hands tremble and her cheeks color.

FROM THE way Lily shot him glances, he knew she felt his presence as much as he sensed hers. He settled back against the side of the front window where he would be out of the way and yet could see everything. Customers came through the door to add to the crowd until only his height let him watch how she turned scowls into smiles.

Lily took a harassed young mother in hand, picked up the woman's boy to ride on her hip, and showed her what they had on offer, leaving Bettina to take the next request. The other two ran from the kitchen in the back with packages or new trays to replace those that emptied. It could have been chaos. Instead, everything seemed under control.

The patterns of customers asking for and getting packages, paying and making their way out the door, made up an odd performance much like those he'd seen in the theater. From the way the others looked to Lily, Henry felt confident she had orchestrated the approach, one more aspect for him to admire. She might be young in comparison to most who held a position of such responsibility, but she'd clearly earned the title.

His gaze swept the room another time, considering whether he should join the queue or if the bakery would empty out before he drew the ire of his inspector.

The pattern broke.

Not in a big way. Customers continued to make their requests and get their goods. Instead, it was a small action that caught his eye, one he didn't consciously notice until he looked back.

A lanky boy stretched over the counter at the far end and snatched a bun from the tray. From the look of his bulging pockets, he'd done the same move several times already.

Henry didn't have to think.

He pushed off the wall, twisted through the crowd with enough authority so they moved out of his way, and closed a firm hand over the offender's shoulder. "Stealing is against the law. Stealing from good people like these is even worse," he ground out, his tone deep and severe.

The boy shrank in on himself. He knew he'd been caught and made no attempt to twist free.

Henry lowered his brows at the desperate look in the boy's eyes. He had a successful waif-look that may have won him freedom from gullible matrons, but Henry had seen his share of swindlers.

He glanced to Lily, thinking she'd find his effort just as appealing as he'd appreciated her management.

She met his gaze, but her look held more apprehension than pride.

Henry looked at the boy again, trying to see this criminal through Lily's eyes. She was not the type to be taken in by a swindler. She'd proven her mental acuity more than once, and yet she seemed to side with the boy.

The pockets that held what the boy had stolen did not match the tunic they'd been sewed onto with rough stitches. Stains marked the cloth. More than either of those, when he looked beyond the eyes, Henry saw how the boy's skin clung tight to his bones. This was no merchant or nobleman's son out to cause trouble. This boy had seen hardship most would not survive. That he'd not been swept into one of the workhouses could only be a miracle. Henry had seen those places. Desperate children working long hours for less than would sustain someone half their sizes.

His hand released without conscious thought.

Henry dropped to his knees and met the boy's gaze on the same level. "Take yourself down to the station. You know where it is, I suspect." He paused long enough to receive the boy's fearful nod. "You're to ask for Officer Parson. Tell him Sergeant Henry sent you. That he's to find work for you there. No matter how hungry, stealing is wrong. You will work for your keep, or you'll be behind the bars rather than in front of them. Do you understand?"

Again the boy nodded, then both hands thrust into his pockets and he brought forth three dirt-stained buns, his arms shaking as he extended them toward Henry.

Henry looked at the buns and shook his head. No one would buy these, and no purpose could be served in them going to waste. He plucked them from the boy's hands, one of his engulfing all three pieces.

His free hand closed again on the boy's shoulder, but with a much gentler touch. When the customers moved out of his way this time, they moved not because of authority but because they could sense something important occurring.

Henry tried not to feel disappointed at how Lily's skin paled even more as he approached the counter with the boy. He gave her a reassuring smile, then nudged the boy forward. "You owe this woman, this bakery, an apology."

The boy looked from him to Lily, swallowed visibly, and piped out in a voice much higher than a healthy boy should have, "I'm sorry."

Henry gave the boy's shoulder a light squeeze, but did not release him. Instead, he brought his hand with the three buns up into view. "Add these to my order," he told Lily before turning back to the boy. "Straight to the station with you now," he said as he handed over the three buns. "I'll know if you don't, and Officer Henry always gets his man."

The boy's eyes widened, the threat heard and understood, but then his back straightened and he gave a solemn nod, the buns clutched to his chest. By the time he reached the door, though, a bun had already found its way to between his teeth.

Henry watched him leave and scamper down the street until he passed out of view from the bakery windows. Somehow, he knew the boy would go to the station and find Parson. Lily was a great judge of character, and she'd seen what he had not. Unlike how a successful nab left him filled with satisfaction, this time a warmer emotion filled his chest.

WHILE HENRY watched the boy, Lily watched the officer. She'd seen his expression when he seized the thief. In that moment, law had been supreme.

But something had changed. She didn't know what; she didn't understand it.

When he brought the boy to the counter, he'd paid for the stolen buns, but more, he'd trusted the boy to go to the station as directed. He'd shown kindness and understanding where most would have only seen a thief to be punished, an officer more than any other.

She prayed with all her strength that the boy would be at the station when Henry returned. That his faith would be rewarded.

The daydream of another life where she could encourage his interest curled its way into her mind. If he could see the worth in that boy despite catching him stealing, could he maybe see Samantha as the person she was, creative, curious, and endearing, rather than a dreaded Natural?

No other customer approached the counter, all of them just as caught up in his actions as she had been. Lily blushed to think they'd seen her staring. She moved to get Henry the rest of his order, but Kate handed her the wrapped package before she could leave the front.

"Here you go, Officer Henry." Despite her attempt to be brusque, her voice came out soft.

He turned with his beguiling smile, her already weakened resistance melting away at that. His finger lightly brushed the back of her hand as he accepted the package, the touch so gentle she thought she might have imagined it if not for how his gaze held hers. It brought back not him pushing her to reveal the truth but how his arms had closed around her, offering comfort even without knowing why.

"I'll call for you tomorrow at noon."

His deep voice carried, and Lily knew she would be hearing questions about the boy and Henry's plans from customers for the rest of the day. Again, her cheeks heated with no oven nearby to provide an excuse.

"I'll be waiting," she answered, her voice hardly above a whisper. She glanced to where Bettina kept the other girls back, but could not tell which of them had given him her direction.

He laid his coin on the counter and gave her another of his dimpled smiles. "'Til the morrow, then, Miss Lily."

She couldn't bring herself to move, to return to all the customers and tasks that lay in wait. From where she stood, she watched Henry as he went out the door and down the street, his determined stride broken only as he ducked around two boys playing hoops then paused to help an older woman bring her packages to the waiting steam carriage.

Lily knew better than to expect anything from his interest. Had her life been different, had her father still lived, perhaps his attentions might have become something more, but whereas the distance between a member of the peerage and a well-off merchant's daughter could be breached on the rare occasion, a much greater gulf stood between a viscount and a shop girl, not even considering her orphaned status.

She shook her head, unable to believe what she'd been contemplating. His intentions had no importance at all when she considered her state. But that didn't stop her from wishing things were different.

"Now I know for sure you have feelings for the man," Jane said, nudging Lily to one side so she could reach the loaves of bread beneath the counter where Lily stood. "I wouldn't have thought anything could make you neglect the customers."

Lily glanced around her in shock. She had forgotten those still waiting to be served, something that had never happened before.

Instead of irritated expressions, though, her gaze found Bettina helping one woman, Kate off with another, and one waiting patiently for Jane. The other girls had done their best work and cleared the crowd until they had some breathing room.

Lily took the payments automatically, none of the purchases out of the ordinary, but her thoughts kept drifting to where they should not have gone. Henry had become as much of a fixture in her mind as he had in the bakery.

Once the room stood clear of customers, the younger girls gathered at the counter to tease.

"You needn't worry one bit, Lily. It's clear he returns your feelings in full measure. A blind fool could see he's smitten."

If Lily's cheeks burned any hotter, she'd faint as though in the grasp of a fever. "You forget just who he is. And who I am," she said, as much to remind herself as them.

"Now, girls." Bettina swept in for the rescue before they could dismiss the difference, all caught up in romantic tales, and took both Kate and Jane with her. "Our Lily doesn't need the likes of you to tell her what's what. She's the first to recognize the worth in any man or woman."

Lily followed Bettina's example and set about replacing the baked goods that had sold through the morning. If the trays looked too bare, customers would think the remaining wares old and stale. The task offered little distraction for her mind, though, and she half wished the girls were right about his interest, though it would never turn into an actual courtship, even if he desired one.

She slotted the last tray into place and picked up the cleaning cloth she kept near the main counter. With broad strokes, she scrubbed the counter free of crumbs that were as imaginary as any future different than what she had planned. Memory of this moment, of her feelings within it, would have to keep her warm on many a lonely night without even her sister to keep her company.

The outing with Henry would be needlessly cruel when she could never accept another, both to him and to her, but she'd done what she could to end it and failed. Now, she would have to tell her sister she could not stay long in the morning, and she'd do her best to wring every drop of enjoyment from the flower market. Fate would not be so kind as to send her another like Henry once England lay behind them and her sister was happily ensconced in a safe haven.

CHAPTER 16

Henry stamped his feet and rubbed his hands together, the cold night making a lie of the morning's break in winter weather. He considered attempting to overcome Lily's silence on their outing, but could not chance harm coming to her on this night because he chose not to come.

The chime from the bakery door gave warning, and Henry pulled back so she wouldn't catch sight of him watching. All the other girls had left much earlier, a pattern he'd noticed before he'd spoken to her that first time, one designed, he now felt sure, to hide her secret.

Despite her calm efficiency earlier in the day, she paused and stared about before stepping free of the door, looking like nothing less than a scared rabbit.

His heart ached for her.

Lily worked such long hours, and yet when they came to an end, rather than rushing to a welcoming home, she hesitated. He'd teased the location of her lodgings from the bakery girls, and that she lived with the sister of Mr. Cooper's housekeeper, all the more reason to keep her reputation pure. The house stood in a decent, if run-down, neighborhood, but neither it nor the careful repairs he'd noticed in her clothing matched what Mr. Cooper must have been paying her. He would bet a month's earnings from his holdings that what made her so nervous when leaving the bakery had the same cause as her apparent lack of funds.

Henry glanced away, uncomfortable in his observation of her low moment, only to have his gaze fall on a steam cart rounding the corner opposite to Lily's direction.

"Make way. Make way."

While more often than not such a cry signaled a thoughtless aristocrat, the edge of panic in this voice jerked Henry's focus to the grim-faced driver perched above the unstable cart. It swayed from side to side as it bore down on him, the top so covered in ornamentation that it carried more weight than the chassis could support at those speeds.

It rebounded off a gas lamp's pole not that far from where Henry sheltered and lurched toward the other side of the street where Lily stood frozen by the sight.

Forgetting stealth, forgetting everything else, Henry dove across the street and shoved Lily back into the bakery doorway just in time as the steam cart smashed against the entryway supports, barely missing the window which would have showered them with glass.

Lily held tight in his arms, Henry watched the cart tip, seem to right itself, then begin to topple as though time itself had slowed. The ornamentation came to rest on the cobblestones first with a brittle crunch as the remainder of the transport's weight sank upon it, pipes bursting with a gust of hot, damp air.

Henry knew he should go check on the driver and any other occupants, but Lily leaned back, the terror fading from her eyes and a trembling smile on her lips.

Everything else faded in importance.

"Thank you, Henry." She paused as though equally aware she'd used his given name, and added in a soft whisper. "I could have been under that contraption."

He freed a hand to smooth down her hair where his coat had disordered it, enjoying the sight without the white mob cap she always wore in the bakery. "Don't even think that way. I hope I'll always be here to rescue you."

A frown line creased her brow. "Why are you here? Surely your shift at the station was over long ago? Don't you ever rest?"

Warmth spread through him as she showed concern over his person. He touched her hair again, as much for the pleasure as to buy some time to concoct an answer. "I'm on a case in the neighborhood," he said, sticking as close to the truth as he could manage. "It's luck— or fate—that brought me to your rescue."

She shook her head, but a smile softened the denial. "Whatever the cause, I'm grateful for it. Still, shouldn't you be checking on the man in that steam cart?"

Henry followed her gaze to where a man, gentleman from his dress, had pulled himself free of the wreckage. After circling the fallen cart twice, the man came to a halt and stood shaking his head.

"He looks fine to me. Better than he should be, considering he's the cause of this accident. It's you who's still trembling."

Lily glanced up at him as though unaware of the tremors in her arms until he mentioned them. "I wasn't expecting something like this to happen here, especially not so late at night. But I came to no harm. I'm just shaken."

Henry looped her arm through his. "Then I shall walk you home. See you safely to your own doorstep." The realization that this would mean yet another day wasted in uncovering her troubles came only after his offer. Perhaps he would need to question her at the flower market after all.

"Oh." She pulled her hand free. "I couldn't ask you to do that. I'm fine. A walk in the night air and any lingering effects will vanish. Besides, don't you have some duty to that fellow? To bring him to task for the danger he provided if nothing else."

"I'm off—" Henry swallowed his words in time to prevent contradicting his earlier statement that he was on a case, but still she turned an inquiring gaze on him. "...to do just that. It won't take but a moment. Are you sure I can't walk you home afterwards?"

Lily shook her head and gave him a gentle smile before waving Henry to the task he had no wish to perform. "I walk this way every night. I'll be fine."

He had no choice but to watch her leave.

His duty reasserted itself with the affect of her presence lifted. He strode over to the gentleman. "You all right over here, Sir?" The title was required by the uniform Henry wore, if not his social standing, and he preferred to keep the two separate.

"Dash it all, no, I'm not fine. I'm in a heap of trouble. Aunt Millie's steam cart all overset and on my first run with the blasted thing. She'll have my hide for this."

Henry closed a hand on the man's arm, laying claim to his full attention. "You're lucky that's all this venture cost you. You almost took down a young woman in your fall. Let this be a lesson to you. Steam carts are no different than a matched pair. You have to keep them in hand, especially in town."

The young man turned to stare at the wreckage. "Right you are, Gent. I'll never hear the end of this."

On any other day, Henry would have brought this man back to the station on charges of disturbing the peace, property damage, and endangering innocents. This night, however, the thought of Lily walking on to whatever dangers awaited her while still jumpy from the near accident plagued him.

"I'll let you off with a warning, but I better not see that steam cart involved in any other accidents with you on the seat."

The gentleman turned to face Henry fully for the first time, taking in the uniform coat and boots, all that were visible in the cold. "Oh. I didn't realize. I'm sorry, Officer. Yes, I swear. You'll not find me on the seat of that monstrosity at another accident or any other time."

Henry gave the man a stiff nod of dismissal, despite the unsatisfactory wording that failed to account for the man's own responsibility. "You'll need to secure help in righting this. If it's still here come morning, I will track you down to account for the mess."

With that, he turned and strode away, wasting no more time as he followed after Lily. She couldn't have gotten far, not in her state. Even without her troubles, the roads had become treacherous with the earlier warmth melting any remaining snow so it refroze into ice with the deeper night cold. Who knew how many other steam carts or carriages would be driving too fast on the slick cobblestones?

He pushed away the consequences of a second rescue when she'd refused his escort. He would deal with any should they come up. From what he'd learned, she had no one, no father and no mother, to care for her. It wasn't right for a thoughtful, caring young woman like herself to be alone in the world. Whether she'd have him or no, Henry had appointed himself her guardian. He suspected Fitz had been right after all, and someday soon, he would ask her for more.

THE WARMTH of Henry's body, the strength of his arms around her, lingered as Lily continued on her way to the stable. She'd grown tired of standing all on her own. These moments with Henry brought that truth to the forefront no matter how hard she tried to bury it. She wanted someone to share both the bad times and the good should she eventually reach them. Someone to lean on as much as she would offer them support.

Her sister could never be that person.

Samantha would never be able to live a normal life here, and because of that, Lily would never have the chance either.

Instead, she would take Sam to the Continent and what passed for a normal life with others like her. Lily, though, would have no more place there than Samantha had here in England.

Her shoulders curved, against a rush of bitter wind, or so Lily told herself. She trudged the final distance, forgetting her plan to go a different route each day until the last moment when she took the second street rather than the first, both with an entrance onto the alley.

HENRY HEADED for where he'd lost sight of Lily the previous time he'd trailed her. The longer he'd listened to the man, the more confident he became that Lily would not skip her nightly meeting despite the near disaster. He should have stayed—in any other circumstances, he would have—but this could be his best chance to discover just who put the fear in Lily's eyes.

The hunch took him scrambling down the path she'd taken that first night. When he arrived at the mouth of the alley to find it empty, though, he almost turned away, sure he'd missed her a second time.

Luck was with him, and he caught a glimpse of Lily before he could stride away. She came toward him from the far end when she'd gone in from this side the previous time.

He ducked across the street to a doorway from which he could watch the opening, but instinct told him she would not be coming out any time soon.

CHAPTER 17

L ily, Lily, come see, come see."

Samantha greeted Lily barely in the door, but she didn't have the heart to scold her sister, not after she'd spent the walk consumed by disloyal thoughts. "What is it, Sam?"

Her sister's head popped out of the tack room and she waved Lily in. "I taught the metal man to climb and be an acrobat like that circus Father took us to."

Lily stared at her sister, amazed Samantha even remembered anything from the circus. She'd been so young. Then the mechanical man's antics caught Lily's attention instead.

Despite his still metal parts, through some wonder of engineering closer to magic than anything a normal person could construct, the little mechanical climbed a rope onto an improvised stage. It went through movements very close to those of the acrobats at the circus, each executed with precision, and a measure of grace.

"That's incredible, Sam."

Her sister didn't turn as she clapped for the mechanical man. If her grin had stretched a fraction wider, it would have split her face.

Though the mechanical continued its performance, Lily watched Samantha instead.

The joy in that little form, the pride in her accomplishment, and sweet pleasure in the gift she'd given this creature of metal and springs, showed Sam to be a caring, special person who didn't deserve what fate had thrown her way. Lily had been so sure using the Natural abilities would make the craving worse. She'd held back anything that might have triggered a bout, isolating Samantha and even refusing to speak of the devices she'd seen.

Samantha seemed content to tinker with this one mechanical. There were no signs of the fevers that drove her sister to seek out more and more to transform. Whether a consequence of the mechanical man's complexity, or the touch of another Natural when Sam had never met one of her kind, Samantha seemed happy.

The last of Lily's discontent melted away in the face of her love for her sister. If that love meant making sacrifices, Lily was strong enough to bear them, and bear them alone. She wouldn't risk her sister for anything, certainly not the siren call of a normal life. When Sam had reached a safe haven would be soon enough for Lily to find her own way.

"Did you like it?"

Samantha's question jerked Lily back to the present. She saw the mechanical man making his way back down the rope more like a spider than a person, though he had only two legs and two arms. "Yes, Sam. It was beautiful. Much like the circus as you said."

A quick smile, and Samantha's mind had moved on to other things. "What mechanicals did you see today?"

Her thoughts still caught up in the idea that her sister was improving the mechanical man—not changing him but fixing and bettering him—Lily's mind veered to the poorly balanced steam cart. As she'd been leaving, she'd heard the start of Henry's conversation with the young man who'd almost run them down.

"I was in the shop all day, and if any passed, I didn't notice." She wondered if Sam would like the story of the boy, but decided she'd spoken too much of Henry as it was, especially with abandoning her sister for her day off. If having a mechanical didn't start the fevers, maybe speaking of the steam cart wouldn't either. "As I left, though, I was almost bowled over by an out-of-control steam cart."

"Really? Why did the mechanism act that way?"

A jolt of laughter burst from Lily at the thought of steam carts that drove themselves. "Steam carts aren't like your mechanical man, Sam. They have human drivers just like any other carriage. Only there are no horses to pull them."

Samantha nodded as though she understood, but Lily could almost see the thoughts churning in her little head as she worked out just how a horseless carriage would function, and how the driver would control it.

"This one had been plastered with so much ornamentation, it swayed top-heavy," Lily added, hoping to distract her sister from the hows. Perhaps telling Samantha about this hadn't been the best idea after all. "It jumped the curb and tried to crush me into the wall."

That caught Samantha's attention and the little girl gasped. "How ever did you duck out of the way?"

Lily couldn't help her smile even as she realized this story came back to Henry as much, if not more so, than that of the boy. "Henry saved me," she said, forgetting the Officer title again. "He was passing by and saw the steam cart before I did." Again, his warmth comforted her, though the memory held little weight compared to the reality of his touch.

"You like this Henry?"

The question startled Lily. Samantha's sheltered upbringing hardly made her aware of normal relationships, and she surely didn't understand how complicated the query was even without the trouble Henry's professional calling would bring. To Samantha, Lily's feelings about Henry must have been the same as her sister's like for the mechanical man. Lily could find no way to answer such an innocent question.

"If you like him, you should marry him. Then I would have a papa again, and you wouldn't be so lonely when you have to leave here. We could go somewhere and live as a family, the three of us."

Lily stared at her sister, at the smug look on Samantha's face as though she had solved the world's problems when everyone else seemed blind to them.

"You don't understand how it is outside these walls, Sam. I can't just marry some gentleman and go off to the Continent come spring." Especially not a police officer, but she didn't say that part aloud.

"I wouldn't have to be a secret. He could come with us. It would be a grand adventure. Or maybe I wouldn't have to go at all."

Samantha's voice held the same overly patient tone Lily recognized from when she'd had to convince her sister of something, but there was so much Samantha didn't understand. They'd never set foot on a boat if she told Henry the truth. There would be no Continent, no safe haven, nothing more to worry about ever because they'd both be locked up.

Her chest tightened until drawing a breath took effort, and her heart beat a ragged rhythm, but sharing that fear would help no one. Let Samantha have her illusions. She'd never meet Henry, so she'd never have to know how even a kind gentleman with strong ethics would turn on her.

Lily thrust a hand into her cloak, remembering the treat she had for Samantha now, when it offered the perfect distraction. "The bakery was so busy this morning that some pastries stayed in the oven too long. I brought you the one that was my share. Why don't you try it while I put together our dinner?"

Samantha's eyes widened as she stared at the pastry. "You didn't burn it, did you?"

That surprised a laugh. "No, Kate was managing the ovens, but it could have been any of us what with how many customers crowded the front. Go ahead and enjoy it. Mr. Cooper knows this can happen a time or two. It's only a worry if something always gets burnt."

Despite all the things that set her sister apart from other children, a love of sweets rose strong in the little girl. She didn't need further comment to draw the pastry close and savor every aspect of the rare treat.

Lily swallowed a relieved sigh as her offering served its purpose. Samantha had lost all interest in pursuing a topic that had no good outcome, no matter what Lily's daydreams proclaimed. Lily chose not to remind her sister of the planned outing either. Henry spent too much time in her thoughts. She need not infect her sister with the same condition.

WAITING HAD been part of his training, both with his brother and the force. Waiting for something to happen, waiting for a sneak thief to return to the scene, and even waiting for his next assignment.

He'd never cared so much about what rode on his patience before now.

Henry rolled his shoulders then clutched his coat tighter against the chill wind. He stamped his feet.

Finally, unable to wait a moment longer, he launched himself across the street, knowing if Lily caught him there, she would reject his assistance a second time, but worse, she would reject him.

He had no choice, not and live up to who he wanted to be.

Henry strode down the alley, finding just what he'd expected.

On one side, a brick wall stretched the whole length without a single opening. On the other, though, he found a simple wood door that must have led into the dilapidated stables.

What better place to hide criminal activities than somewhere everyone had grown used to seeing but which no longer had a purpose in this new, steam-infused society.

Henry paced the stretch of alley, but neither side offered a place to tuck himself into. He fought the urge to burst in and rescue her from whomever drew her to this place.

He was too good an officer not to know the plan had little value. There could be anywhere from one to two dozen men arrayed against him beyond that door, the wind, even here, loud enough to muffle any noises from within. And with Lily in their command, they'd have leverage to use against him. His only choice was once again to wait it out, no matter how long this took, until Lily made it to safety.

Though sympathetic with the men whose living had been stolen by the steam revolution, Henry could not condone these enterprises. They had little to do with earning a wage. Another group had taken roost on his beat a month past, blackmailing young women in all manner of ways to get them to hand over a share of their earnings.

It took but a whisper in the wrong ear to ruin a woman's reputation, and the jobs a tainted girl could find offered little in the way of coin or security.

His steps dragged as he trudged back out of the alley and returned to the spot that made the whole length visible. Whichever end she left by, he would see her go. It did neither Lily nor her tormenters any good if a late arrival at her rooms caused the very thing they threatened.

When he had confirmed she'd gained a safe distance, he would put an end to this sorry business once and for all.

He didn't have to wait much longer, though.

As he settled as best he could into the alcove, the side door swung open, leaking only a faint glimmer of light into the alley, but still bright enough to dazzle his dark-adjusted eyes. A moment earlier, and he'd have been caught in the open and vulnerable.

He blinked to clear his vision in time to see Lily glance back the way she'd come, as though more afraid of what she left inside than the weather or any ruffians who might be passing by.

After a moment, she shut the door firmly and started toward him at a brisk pace.

Henry froze, thinking she'd seen him, but then she turned at the corner and kept going, oblivious to his presence.

Part of him wanted to follow her, to see her safely home as he'd promised, but he'd never have a better opportunity to address the situation with her tormenters. For all he knew, they came here only to meet victims like Lily and would be scattered to the wind should he bring a team down on them in the day. No one had gone with her, and none had left since Lily escaped the building. The likelihood of another side entrance seemed slim, and he could see both the main one and the one Lily used. Experience told him they'd be busy inside, counting out the portions of Lily's hard-earned wages.

He looked first to ensure Lily had passed far enough that she wouldn't notice him moving, then Henry detached himself from the hiding spot. He strode across the street, rolling his shoulders to release any tension built up in his wait at the same time as he pulled forth his baton.

Unlike many of the officers, a gentleman's childhood meant he'd had training in many more ways to take down an opponent than brute force, but the sight of a policeman's baton worked for intimidation as well as use.

He paused, one hand on the latch, to take a deep breath. Beyond this point, he could face a dozen or more hardened men, men who thought plaguing young women a better way to keep themselves than an honest living. Even if their livelihood had been stolen by the very steam revolution Henry tried to keep in check, they had little respect for their fellows, and likely less even for the law. Whatever sympathies he might hold, he could not condone what they had done and planned to stop them whatever it took.

His grip on the baton firmed, and he jerked the door open wide to get the best view possible.

"Lily? Did you forget something?"

Henry froze at the high-pitched, child's voice. His mind stumbled over itself in an effort to realign his thoughts. He jammed the baton back under his coat and smoothed his scowl into the smile he offered to Lily at the least chance.

Just in time.

A sturdy girl rounded the corner and stopped dead.

Henry swept a bow, dying of curiosity but unable to ask just who she was and what she meant to Lily without being unforgivably rude. "Henry Stapleton at your service."

As she moved closer, he could see a faint resemblance to Lily despite their different builds. The girl must have been large for her age, because the answer to Lily's secret, though he doubted the bakery girls knew it, now seemed obvious.

"Are you Lily's Henry?"

He stifled a laugh at the jolt of happiness her innocent question offered him. He'd made enough of an impression that Lily mentioned him to her...what? Illegitimate child? No wonder Lily hid the girl here. If this were to get out, she'd lose her good position and the reputation necessary to get another.

Society might frown on an unwed mother, but Henry had seen enough as a police officer to know life didn't always turn out the way a person might expect. For her to have chosen this life over dropping her newborn on the steps of a foundling home showed a depth of love and strength most wouldn't share. No wonder she'd seen the child in Tom, as the boy was called, when he'd seen only a thief.

The girl tipped her head to one side. "Is it so hard a question?"

Henry pushed away his thoughts to focus on the girl. "No. No, not a hard question. It's just complicated."

The girl let out a sigh almost bigger than she was. "That's what Lily always says." Her face brightened. "So you must be her Henry. Come on."

Before he could extract himself from the situation, not that he wanted to, the girl wrapped her fingers around his hands and tugged him deeper into the stables.

"I'm Sam. Samantha really, but Lily calls me Sam. And this is my home."

The stable tack room held a table, two chairs, a bed, a stove, and a couple of toys scattered around the room.

Samantha dropped his hand to scurry across the floor and pick one of them up, whispering to it before tucking the toy away behind her bed.

Henry supposed he'd be talking to his things as well if he lived in such a stark situation. Maybe some would think Samantha better off in a foundling home with real friends, but they didn't know how harsh that life could be. He wouldn't either except he'd had to return a foundling runaway once. The boy now worked on Henry's estate. Overworked staff, even those with kindness in their hearts, could offer little cheer while money was tight so the food had little enough nutrition and the orphans fought over it.

"So," Samantha said, coming to stand next to him. "Did you bring anything? Why are you here? Lily says no one's supposed to know." A scowl as intense as the one he'd planned to confront Lily's tormenters with took over the little girl's face. "You're not supposed to be here, are you?"

Henry shrugged and tried for an innocent smile. "I just wanted to know why Lily seemed so afraid."

He didn't know what he expected next. Still, the sharp nod Samantha gave surprised him.

"I told her I wouldn't have to be a secret." She blinked and scrambled across the room so quickly Henry wondered if she thought to escape him. But she went to the table instead, climbing onto the nearest chair. "Would you like some of my pastry?"

He looked at the offering, one side nibbled and much of the rest showing burnt edges, clearly discarded as worthless. About to refuse so Samantha could keep her gift, Henry met the hope in the girl's eyes and found himself saying, "I'd love a bite or two."

"Grand." As fast as she'd gone to the table, now she came back and caught his hand, dragging him over. "Lily says we must eat in chairs…like proper people."

He said nothing as they both sat down, or rather, Samantha knelt. She reached for what must have been a rare treat and tore a piece off to hand to him. He thought of what he'd seen at the foundling house and knew Lily had done better for her daughter than giving her up would have done. To share so easily meant both a kind nature and the knowledge that she wouldn't starve for it.

Henry took the smallest possible bite. He wanted to extend this moment, to get to know the part of Lily's life she thought she had to hide.

He glanced around the room again, this time with different eyes. Instead of the barren space, he noticed a hand-stitched blanket and a doll he'd missed that rested on the bed next to a well-stuffed pillow. His gaze returned to the delight in Samantha's expression as she delicately devoured the rest of her pastry between sending him crumb-filled grins.

Samantha might spend much of her time alone, and welcomed the chance at company, but there was no question the little girl knew she had all the love in the world.

"Can we play a game? Lily plays with me when she can, but she comes so late and just can't stay. We haven't had time for reading either."

He could no more have refused that imploring look than the pastry she'd offered so generously. Henry could see trouble brewing in the future if he didn't develop a backbone where this child was concerned. He suspected he'd be spending as much time here as he could manage, though he hoped for Lily's permission.

As they played, he listened to her chatter and watched her choices, each moment strengthening his feelings for Lily. He might not have been sure of his path before, but now he resolved to take on not only the young woman who had taken up residence in his heart but her unique and fascinating little girl as well.

Let society think what it might about illegitimate children and the women who bore them. There'd be many who would question Lily's ability to function as a lady, too. Somehow, Henry felt confident she could find her way there as easily as she managed the chaos in the bakery, and he vowed to make sure no taint would darken the lives of this entrancing girl or her equally exceptional mother.

CHAPTER

18

Henry had made arrangements to switch his day off with Parson after admitting to his plans and receiving another dour lecture. He'd spent the morning pacing as he suffered both anticipation and fear. How would Lily react to his discovery? He could understand now why she didn't want to risk telling him or anyone. Like a wolf with cubs, she protected her own, yet another admirable quality.

By the time he arrived at the townhouse that had been converted into a rooming house, he'd decided to say nothing unless she spoke first. Samantha had agreed to keep their visit a secret, though whether he or she had advanced the idea first, he couldn't quite recall. Still, as precocious as the girl was, Henry knew from the servants' children that decisions made in one moment could be forgotten in the next.

He rang the doorbell and locked his hands behind his back to keep them from rapping against the wall. Depending on whether she'd been to see her daughter this morning, he could receive a delightful greeting or the sound of the door slamming in his face.

"Oh, good. It's you," Lily said as she swung the door open. "I'm leaving now, Mrs. Marsh."

The second she called back into the house as she stepped through the door, preventing any chance of him meeting her landlady, the closest she had to a guardian besides her employer from what he could tell.

Henry took the setback in hand along with Lily and helped her into his steam cart though she gave it a wary eye.

"I swear to you I can handle this as good as any matched pair. I thought it might do better where we're going."

She flashed him a smile that only trembled on the edges.

Her swift comprehension that to bring horses down where those of many stations were present would set them uncomfortably apart only made him appreciate her more.

As he navigated the streets, careful to watch for obstacles, the silence weighed heavy. Henry fought the need to blurt out his visit with Samantha, unsure whether that or the unusual conveyance stilled her tongue. He needed to show her he could be trusted, prove it to her, before she'd open up to him.

"How long have you been working at Cooper's Bakery?" he said at last, unable to bear the tension, though she seemed not to feel it at all.

Lily turned to look at him, eyes sparkling. "Since I was sixteen. My father's work had no place for me, and Mr. Cooper has no children, so they thought it the answer to both concerns."

That broke through the barrier between them, and soon Henry shared as many stories of Robert as Lily did from her childhood. She paused at points, especially in mention of the sister she'd lost, but Henry did not pry, showing himself willing to listen without probing.

As they pulled up to the area set aside for carts, Lily seemed more relaxed than he'd ever seen her. Henry vowed to push all other considerations aside and focus on giving Lily a memorable outing. Her life had suffered many changes. She deserved a moment of peace without worry.

FIRST THE cart glided through the streets, its faint click of gears and hiss of steam so quiet it felt almost as though magic conveyed them along, like the wild tales from the East of floating carpets. Then Henry took her into the flower market, a place transformed for the winter.

Glass panels encased in thick metal frames enclosed a street that stood open in the summer. Moist heat welcomed them from the chill, but even those wonders couldn't surpass the flowers themselves.

Tables stood on every side, an attendant ready to cut flowers from the blooming pots arrayed on shelves behind them. Where summer meant the flowers lay ready, these were given the best chance at survival, and at prices to match. More wandered the halls to admire as she did than to purchase, though there were many of those as well, generally dressed in crisp livery.

Lily paused to watch as a flower seller sliced through the stems, laid the flowers out, then rolled them into a thick cloth. The woman dipped her wrist onto the surface of several pots of standing water before choosing one to soak the cloth in and added another layer. From the steam rising above the farthest, the flowers were given lightly heated water to maintain their beauty as they were carried off to whatever household had ordered them.

Though some purchased whole pots, the sellers seemed reluctant to part with the plants themselves, indicating the chance of a second or even third flowering in this protected environment.

Henry kept at her side, pointing out what he observed and no less intrigued by the process as far as she could tell.

He continued to surprise her at every turn. That he believed in upholding the law could not be questioned. But he'd chosen to give the boy a chance. He cared little for the differences in their station. He chose to take her here rather than commanding her presence at some event frequented by the peerage, and he delighted in the simple wonders around him.

Not once had he pressed her since the time in the bakery. When they spoke, he held nothing back, speaking honestly of his brother and their rivalry, then of his sorrow at losing every remaining member of his family in one deadly stroke. He listened when she told of her own family and did not pry into the details of her sister's death.

The urge to tell him about Samantha rose once again.

He did not gossip. He understood events could be more complex than the law would hold them to be. His worth he'd shown more times than could be counted, to her and to everyone he met it seemed.

Still, she kept silent. The secret was not hers alone to share. No matter how much she thought him capable of seeing beyond what everyone believed to be true about Naturals, no matter how much he overcame all sorts of limits set between people, she would not risk Samantha just to ease her own isolation.

Samantha had been in rare form this morning, more joyful even than when the mechanical man came into her life despite how little time Lily could spare for her. Again, her sister spoke of Henry as a father figure, something that colored Lily's perceptions whenever she looked on him as they admired the colorful growths, so different from the gray chill outside of this place.

Here, Lily could imagine a chance for them, surrounded by impossible flowers when spring would not come for a long time still. Here, she could pretend Samantha would find a staunch advocate in Henry and she'd find a helpmate.

Henry strode toward the entrance, a clear signal their day had come to an end, or so she thought until he paused before one of the tables displaying flowers of many colors and types they'd stopped at earlier.

Lily pushed aside her fanciful thoughts to rush after him, but unless she wanted to do an undignified scramble, she'd trail in his wake.

When she reached the table, Henry had already purchased a large, white lily. He handed the wrapped flower to her with a heart-stopping smile.

"Oh, Henry. You shouldn't have. It will die as soon as we step outdoors."

He closed her fingers around the wrapped stem. "We have the steam cart. The flower is set to stay strong long enough to get back to your lodgings. If your landlady will let you, keep it in the kitchen where it's warmer, and it should last a while."

Lily felt the color rise in her cheeks as she gave him a shy smile.

"And the blush on your skin makes the flower worth every bit of its cost. If it keeps the memory of this day in your mind for a little longer, I'm grateful for it. Like the flower, this outing must end, but I'll have the memory of our day forever."

He tucked her hand over his arm, and they headed to the entrance together. His sentiment rang true for her as well, more so than he intended. She'd enjoyed the outing with Henry by letting go of her fears. So too, she should enjoy what time she had with Samantha before they crossed the Channel and separated forever.

The bakery seemed busier the next day, or perhaps the problem lay in how thoughts of Henry distracted Lily from her work. For once, when she ushered the girls out the door, she lingered not to hide her comings and goings but because there was work still to be done.

She'd smelled the sweet scent of her flower all night despite it being down in the kitchen as Henry suggested. Mrs. Marsh delighted in the gift and wanted to hear every detail of their outing, as though she were a proud mother. Samantha's innocent musings on Henry as a new papa continued to haunt Lily, more so because of how connected she felt to the police officer.

Lily dragged a hand under the edge of her cap, shoving away loose hair as she prepared to leave the bakery.

She'd been so absorbed in what she gave up to protect her sister that she'd never considered how Samantha had been denied as well.

Why wouldn't Samantha want a new papa? She remembered their father well, and most likely missed the time they would spend together sharply. Lily didn't speak of Father much, his loss too strong for her to chance dwelling on it. The journals might have helped, but with the mechanical man, they'd been left in their hiding place for too many nights.

Sam never knew their mother. Lily had been there from the moment she'd come into the world. She'd only ever had Lily and Father, and once her knack developed, she lost all contact with anyone beyond the two of them. No one even knew Sam lived except Lily because of the tale they'd had to put about. To have Henry learn about her would expand Samantha's existence immeasurably, though once they reached a safe haven, her sister would have many to visit with, many more than if she stayed with just Lily and Henry, even supposing Henry could be trusted with such a secret.

The door stuck when Lily tried to close it. Lily leaned back hard to jerk it in place, unable to suppress a shiver at the memory of what had happened the last time she stood in this spot.

"Let me help you."

A tiny squeak escaped Lily as large hands folded around hers and the door snapped into place. She turned the key, reluctant to greet her savior who had been the focus of her thoughts too much of late. He'd become the symbol of everything she couldn't have, and now even what she couldn't give her sister.

"Lily." His low voice rumbled her name as Henry caught her arm and turned her himself, as persistent as ever.

She stretched her lips into a smile and tried to hold him off with a joking, "Why Officer Henry, we really should stop meeting like this or people will talk."

Her attempt at humor died when she met his intense gaze, no hint of frivolity there.

"Lily, you've filled my thoughts since I left you yesterday, and the few moments you spared me in the busy bakery this morning only made my needs clearer. I want you by my side."

She jerked away, her heart thumping an uneven rhythm even as she tried to find the strength to protest. "I'm no man's doxy," she managed, her tone more of a whisper than firm. His words brought up images strong enough to raise the heat of her skin. The thought of binding her life to his, even for a short while, appealed more than she'd ever wanted it to.

His reaction had little to do with expectation. He reared back and stood rigid as he stared down at her with a frown creasing his brow. "You misunderstand my meaning. You have no living parent, or relative to speak of, or I would make my case before them. Lily, I have fallen in love with you. I'm not asking for you to take up residence only in my bed but in my life." He sank to one knee, ignoring how the cold and slush must have seeped into the cloth to chill him.

If anything, his correction made Lily feel worse not better. Her stomach churned at the realization of what he offered, and at how much she wanted to throw herself into his arms and claim his love for her own.

Instead, she pulled at his shoulders, trying to get him to rise. Her efforts had no effect.

"Get up, Officer Stapleton." She used his full title despite circumstances when she longed to give him the answer he wanted. "You must know it's not right, you and I."

She had dreamed of this moment, but had known even then the dream to be false. How could she convince him, though, without revealing why? He'd been raised a man of privilege, used to getting his way.

The last gave her an answer, though her heart cried out at the falsehood. "You are titled. I'm merely a shop girl. We could not be a worse match."

Henry rose at that, but before Lily could relax, he caught hold of both her hands and laced his fingers with hers. "You could not be more wrong about that, Lily. You are so much greater than the position you hold. Everyone knows it. That's why the girls, even Bettina, look to you for answers. You're the lady of your very own manor in that bakery, and you have the ability to be so much more."

She tried to pull her hands free, to turn away. "I'm sorry, Henry. I really am. The answer cannot be yes."

He loosed one hand then caught her chin and forced Lily to face him. "How you say my name gives hope despite your rejection. I know why you hesitate. I know your secret."

Lily froze, her blood becoming ice and her trapped hand trembling in his grasp.

He rubbed her cheek with his thumb pad, the rough texture awakening her nerves. "It's all right. There's no need to fear. I've met your daughter."

A gasp she couldn't stifle escaped Lily's mouth, and she jerked against a hold grown strong as steel.

"No, don't fear me. I don't care about that. Your reputation is safe in my hands. I'll love her as my own, and who will question a viscount? No one will ever know the truth about her birth."

Lily stared at him, frozen for a long moment before her mind caught up with what he was saying. He'd be willing to protect her reputation at the cost of his own, to hide what he believed to be Samantha's taint.

She fought down the desperate laugh that threatened to strangle her.

She'd known all along Henry was a good man. She just hadn't known exactly what that meant, or what he'd be willing to sacrifice for her. If only his understanding had been correct and his sacrifice what she, and Sam, needed.

"Officer Henry." This time her voice came out as firm and sharp as she'd hoped, though the emotion rose from grief. "It's not Sam who keeps us apart. You're wrong about my feelings. I have none for you. I think of you no more than any other customer, or did before you started following me about and confining me at your whim as you do now."

His hand dropped away as she'd known it would, but his eyes narrowed. "All those blushes and smiles? You want me to believe you meant nothing by them?"

Lily could hardly think with his revelation about Sam still pounding in her brain. Samantha would have told her if a man came into the stables, wouldn't she?

Memory of her sister's excitement yesterday morning, one not accompanied with a new display from the mechanical man, rose up to confront her. What if her sister could not settle because she'd had a secret? If Henry had seen the toy when he met her sister, they'd be having a much different conversation, but if Sam had snuck out of the stables and been seen, she'd do anything to keep Lily from knowing.

Unable to craft a complete sentence at first with all this whirling through her head, she firmed her lips and gave a jerky nod. "You were the one to force yourself on me," she added after a moment, knowing the charge one that would strike deep. "You refused to listen when I objected and gave me no choice. Of course I blushed. Who would not in those circumstances?"

He straightened his back and glared down at her, but she knew the moment her dagger hit its mark. A stricken look took over his features at the thought he'd forced himself on her, though he had only to think of their outing to know her words false. But she'd chosen her attack well, striking not just at his pride, but at his sense of what was right.

Lily turned to go, keeping her pace to a steady one despite the fear that curdled her stomach.

Henry said nothing, did nothing to stop her. He couldn't suspect what she must now do any more than he had discovered Samantha's true nature. All of her plans and hopes were now lost. The stable was no longer safe, nor was the bakery or her lodgings. How long would it take before someone as observant as Henry noticed how Samantha didn't think quite like other little girls? How long before he caught sight of the mechanical man?

He might have cared enough for Lily to work his way around accepting an illegitimate daughter. He might be willing to use his title to protect them. But he would never accept a fugitive Natural. A viscount did not remain a member of the police without a firm respect for the law. Helping a boy whose only crime is starvation was nothing compared to what he must believe of Naturals, and what he must have seen in the one he caught.

She passed the corner, her chest tight and tears gathering in her eyes for both the man and the life she left behind. Her feet hit the ground a little harder, a little faster, until she ran as though the whole police force drove at her heels. Whatever coins she'd saved would have to be enough to keep them hidden until she could find work on a ship to the Continent. She would do anything. They had no other choice.

HENRY STARED at her retreating back. He didn't move until long after she'd disappeared from his view.

He'd been so sure, so confident.

Arrogant.

He'd become no better than any other of the nobility. He'd taken her pleasantry as more, forced himself on her when she feared to lose her job if she turned him away. He'd become the very ruffians he'd thought plagued her.

Memory of the day she made the special pastry rose, torturing him with her every look and blush. His mind dragged him through each moment spent in her presence. He saw again the day she found the courage to tease him, and how happy she'd been at the flower market, how they'd shared their amazement at the lush garden on so harsh a winter day.

None of it made sense.

No arrogance could have created her sideways glances when she thought he wasn't looking, or the way she shushed the girls to keep them from revealing her true feelings.

Henry slumped against the rough brick wall. What had he done that so repulsed her in the time since he returned her home with the flower? She'd struck him where he was most vulnerable, at the point of privilege and the people. What had changed between her last smile and the way she cut him at the core?

His fist hit the bricks at the moment he realized exactly what he'd done.

First he'd appeared out of the darkness to startle her rather than announcing himself from a distance, then he'd told her about meeting Sam, about uncovering her deepest secret, by just throwing the information into the middle of his proposal with no explanation at all.

He'd seen the fear in her blanched face when she thought he'd track down her secret, and what had he done? In an effort to protect her, he'd stalked and violated her privacy. Even worse, he'd told her he'd been on a case. He'd lied to her while rummaging in her life as though she were one of the very criminals he sought to protect her from.

His costume, donned to make his proposal at her home, only emphasized the point. His police uniform was the closest to formal dress he had when all others he kept out at his parents' manor along with the trappings of his other life. Only his grandfather's pocket watch travelled easily between the two states.

Henry tapped the bricks again, though with less force this time to protect his bruised knuckles.

The police had no interest in questions of reputation, but she wouldn't know that. Lily was a shop girl as she'd said, no matter what she'd been before her misjudgment, and not a student of the law. She probably thought he would be forced to expose her as a liar at the cost of what little income she had, his proposal nothing more than a ruse.

Part of him wanted to give up, wanted to let Lily go and no longer be a strain for her. But he couldn't face the thought of a lifetime stretched before him absent of her smile or scolding, and despite what she'd said, he believed she felt the same. Regardless, he loved her too much to let her live this way, afraid of the shadows and discovery. That blasted title of his had never served a useful purpose before. For Lily, it could be a shield, a defense against the world, if only she would accept it.

His feet started moving, but toward the stable rather than her home. Whatever crazy plan she may have come up with, Samantha would be at the center of it. He could find Lily there, and he would explain that she had nothing to fear from him.

This time he wouldn't let her accusations of force shake him, not until she truly listened. If once she did, she still wanted to walk away, no matter what it cost him, he would let her. But if her feelings were as strong as he suspected, as strong as those that beat in his chest, she would welcome his proposal once she came to trust it.

Lily reached her home out of breath and took the back stairs so no one would delay her. She'd never had better cause to be grateful for the attic space and its servant entrance.

The lock turned, and she swung her door wide. She looked at the room with different eyes now that she had to leave it behind. No matter how much she'd felt at home here, it held little of herself. She'd hung no needlework on the walls and kept all the watercolors she'd done in what seemed like another life tucked away. Samantha's rough efforts decorated the stable where no one else could see them.

No one could suspect Lily had a relative, and she saw no need to flout that she hailed from a wealthy merchant background, an easier task with everything of value gone to pay her father's debts. Still, she'd have to leave behind the steamer trunk her father had given her, the last of her substantial possessions. She could only bring what she and Samantha could carry—carefully mended clothing and her coin.

Even the drawings would be left behind for others to discover and wonder about just who had lived in this house with them. As much as it pained her, she would have to feed her father's journals to Samantha's stove. Those words would only condemn their father's memory and all who might be mentioned between the covers.

Lily dumped her meager possessions onto the mattress and used the bedding to form an awkward bundle. With luck, she and Sam would be mistaken for laundry women and no one would take a second look.

Her store of coins seemed even smaller than she remembered, but still Lily took the time to extract a week's rent and put it on the bare mattress. Mrs. Marsh was a good soul and did not deserve to be left wanting.

Though her reputation would mean nothing once they discovered she had run off in the night, Lily hoped the payment might give them pause. This small justice might still their tongues and keep the bakery from being tainted by whatever story the household settled on to explain her wild behavior. Perhaps in contemplating Lily's disappearance, Mr. Cooper and her landlady would finally manage to make the connection they both seemed to desire. Someone deserved to wring a happy ending from all of this.

With this portion of her life brought to a close, Lily headed toward the stables and her sister. How she would explain all of this to Samantha, she didn't know, but the time had come to run. They could not hesitate or delay no matter how risky the path they would tread.

Ships to the Continent were rare in midwinter, but the messenger packets always seemed to traverse the path between both landmasses. Those captains might be less likely to ask questions, and willing to accept little for payment, as passengers were rare. Escape seemed a better option than finding a new place to hide, but both held their dangers.

The packets ran in winter because, unlike the standard merchant vessels, they had been tricked out with mechanisms of one type or another to prevent catastrophe from rough water and frequent storms. Some were even capable of breaking through ice due to complex machinery.

Lily swore if Samantha could not keep herself under control, Lily would tie her to the bunk and put out word that the little girl was seasick. She had no choice. And that would only be possible if they found a willing ship in the first place.

Her mind offered up images of the two of them freezing on the docks as they sought a ship. Of being discovered only in the spring thaw. But she didn't know of another stable and suspected Henry would search for a similar place. Just where did they have to go?

Caught up in their dreary hopes, at first Lily didn't recognize the sounds she heard when she tugged the side door to the stables open.

Her sister's laughter had become a frequent visitor in this stark place, a high voice chattering away to the mechanical, but the deeper tones to follow had little to do with gears and springs.

Terror iced Lily's veins and bound her in place. Those faint chances seemed now a shining chest of possibilities which reality had turned to ash.

CHAPTER

21

A gain," Sam demanded, her enthusiasm just the distraction Henry needed after the mess he'd made of proposing to her mother.

He'd never imagined himself a family man, yet another role that was supposed to fall to his brother, but Sam made him long for children so he could see them grow and see them become articulate, enthusiastic youngsters like Lily's daughter had.

Still, he met her plea with an exhausted gasp. "You will not be able to fly no matter how hard or fast I spin you."

He sank to the floor, overwhelmed by memories of his father doing the same for him.

"I could fly. With the right pieces, I could build wings."

Henry laughed as Sam knelt at his side.

The little girl had none of the shyness found in most of her age, and little of the proprieties bred into the female sort. The last thought came as she started rifling through his pockets with the skill of a sneak thief.

"You won't find wings in my coat, and I didn't think to bring any sweets, so you'll just have to make do with my company."

Her imagination was catching, a clear sign of how she managed to thrive despite such a limited life. And if it meant she lacked social training, better this than the strictures to bind a creative mind like hers.

Henry glanced toward the door, wondering what was keeping Lily. He wanted to share his delight with her, to prove he meant every word about accepting Samantha. Every strength in Sam only pointed to the wealth of love in Lily, and her weaknesses seemed few.

The faint chink of a watch chain brought his attention back to Lily's daughter. "Now be gentle. That's my grandfather's watch."

He lifted Sam's searching fingers away from his pockets and drew forth the watch on his own, popping it open to check how much time had passed since Lily left him standing in the street.

He'd expected to find her here already, but even when that proved false, Henry had thought she'd come faster than this. Could he have been wrong in thinking she would come to Samantha?

"Can I see it?"

Henry looked up to catch sight of the open longing on Sam's face, her fingers stretched toward him as though pulled by a magnetic force.

"I guess you don't have much in the way of jewelry, now do you? Though this is a man's watch, not a lady's." She was different in so many ways, but it seemed she shared the longing after shiny metal he'd noticed among noblewomen.

He held the polished gold case out so she could get a good look, but kept a firm grasp on it.

Her eyes seemed to glitter as much as the gold when she feasted on the sight.

"Can I touch it?"

Henry hesitated only a moment before shrugging. After all, she'd known to ask politely. "Just be careful. It's been in my family for a long time. I'd hate to have anything happen to the watch."

If she made a response, he didn't hear it as Sam lifted the watch from his palm, and before he could react, popped the back open to see the works with the skill of a master watchmaker.

CHAPTER 22

ily had crept her way to the door, peering in to see the two of them together, laughing and talking as though they'd known each other a lifetime.

Her heart swelled with the realization that he'd spoken the truth. He would have loved Samantha as his own. Henry was a good man, a righteous one, and did not deserve what would happen when Sam let her control slip.

Lily heard Samantha's voice grow louder and faster, saw her sister pat down his chest, but it wasn't until the moment Henry withdrew the watch that tension swept every muscle in Lily's body.

The watch back popped free before she could decide what to do.

Lily dropped her bundle and ran into the tack room, but neither she nor Henry's outstretched hand could make a difference. The bout had already begun.

Samantha's eyes glittered with the fever that took hold of her. The watch chain swung free to dangle on Henry's chest. Gears lifted from the back as though by magic, the little girl's fingers so quick and nimble they were invisible to the eye. What tools appeared must have come from any number of bits of metal scattered about the failed stables. Sam had made some to work on the mechanical man, though now she seemed to have more.

Nothing would stop her sister now, certainly not the fact that Henry was a police officer who would destroy them both.

A swiftly indrawn breath from Henry revealed it too late for Lily to hide the truth, though only a blind man would remain ignorant of Samantha's nature.

With him trapped by the wonder of creation, she knew what she had to do.

He'd seen Samantha. He knew just what she was.

No longer some illegitimate child to be protected in his eyes, he knew her to be a Natural full grown into her abilities. Despite what Lily thought of him, or about him, Henry would uphold the law. That was his purpose, and if ever she'd known a man driven by purpose, it was Henry.

She grabbed a fallen board, one of the many tucked into the corners of this space. Wood splinters bit into her fingers, a just punishment for the use she planned to make of it.

Lily drew back and swung the board at Henry's head with as much force as she could muster. Her arms ached with the blow, a counterbalance to the pain in her heart, as he sank to one side and landed on the dirt floor with a thud.

There was no time to check and make sure he was only stunned, that she hadn't somehow killed him.

Every minute they wasted was one closer to being caught.

The board fell from her numb fingers and hit the ground with a sharp crack. Lily ran the few steps to her sister and grabbed Samantha by the arm, dragging her toward the stable door.

Her sister kept transforming the heirloom watch, oblivious to everything else around her.

IF HE hadn't caught sight of movement in the corner of his eye and understood what he heard to be running steps, Henry would have been knocked unconscious by the blow to his head. As it was, though he shifted at the last second so his shoulder took the brunt of it, still his ears rang and his eyes clouded with tears.

He lay on the dirt floor, dazed and blinking to restore his sight so he could understand what had happened.

His vision cleared at a glacial pace, allowing a vague picture to form before him.

Lily, his quiet, gentle, shy love, now dragged Sam past him toward the door. No one else was in the room. No one else could have struck him.

Henry threw out a hand to stop them, wrapping his fingers around Lily's ankle when he found skin. It was too cold out there. Lily and Sam had no other place to go.

The force of their movement almost wrenched Henry's already sore shoulder out of its socket, but his grunt of pain vanished under Lily's startled cry.

If he'd been quicker, he would have been able to soften their fall. Instead, he could only watch as Lily dropped to the ground, Sam tumbling after in a muddle of arms, legs, and cloth.

He ran his gaze over the two of them to see if they'd come to any harm, but the sight of Samantha arrested his thoughts.

Legs twisted between her sister's, Sam kept playing with his watch as though nothing out of the ordinary had occurred.

Time slowed to molasses as he stared at the little girl, vaguely aware of Lily trapped by the same fascination.

Everything had happened so quickly.

He'd had no time to think from the moment Sam laid hold of his watch.

Now, though, Henry realized just what he'd seen, and what Samantha must be.

The knowledge clashed with what he knew, what he'd been told, and even what he'd seen with his very own eyes, but how else could he explain the transformation occurring before him?

Images of Naturals he'd encountered before, both at the asylum and his recent capture, rose in his mind. Pale, listless, lifeless until a gearbox was brought within their reach. Trapped in a barely human state, grasping at the nearest metal without thought or speech. Seeing them made it easy to follow the law and protect innocent folks despite how he wished it could be another way.

Henry sought those features in Sam, dragging through every moment he'd been in her presence. Even now, caught in the clutch of transformation, her visage held only concentration and focus. He saw no sign of insanity, much less of an inhuman nature.

Her tongue escaped the cage of her lips to poke out one side much as Robert's had done when concentrating. Her eyes shone with a fevered joy, but one he'd seen recently enough as Tom realized rather than punishment, he'd been offered a way out of his sorry life.

He could not reconcile this delightful little girl with the monsters he knew as Naturals.

She was too full of laughter. She loved to play and listen to his stories. Who could be so cruel as to put a girl like Sam in an asylum with the other sort?

Henry blinked, his mind frozen as the implications of his last thought came crashing down on him.

This had been why Lily feared him. The reason she rejected his proposal, and why she tried to run even now.

Sam was a Natural in truth, no matter how unlikely that might seem. Sam was a fugitive, and he was an officer of the law.

CHAPTER 23

The rough dirt of the floor ground against Lily's cheek as she lay there, confused. Until her mind washed away the effects of her fall and the impact of Samantha's body on top of her, she couldn't remember just how she came to be there. She tried to squirm upright only to come to a halt against the hold Henry kept on her ankle.

Memory crashed down, and Lily jerked hard, but Henry would not release her ankle. She hadn't the heart to kick him after the earlier attack had failed.

She had failed at everything.

Henry discovered her secret. Lily hadn't protected her sister well enough. Now she'd pay the price for that failure, but no matter what this would cost Lily, Samantha would be the one to suffer more.

She stared at her little sister, as innocent as any of those Henry had sworn to protect.

Sam played with the new toy as though nothing else happened here.

If Henry had any feelings for Lily at all, she could use them for her sister's sake and would. But asking this of him meant going against everything he stood for. No matter how much he professed to love her, ultimately Henry was a man of firm principles.

"There." Samantha's satisfied proclamation broke through a silence filled only with hard breathing.

The new little man stretched its tiny legs toward the floor. Samantha bent to lower it down, her elbow gouging Lily's side.

No sooner than the mechanical's feet touched dirt, it gave a whirl of gears and scampered across the floor under its own power, heading for its true owner no matter what form it held or who had transformed it.

Lily sucked in a breath and stared at Henry.

She'd forgotten just what her sister had taken. Samantha was no innocent in Henry's eyes. She'd taken something from him, and something precious. She was no different than all the other Naturals, taking what didn't belong to them and making it into something it had never been meant to be. Henry's heirloom watch might still tell time, but he could never use it again, not where it might be seen.

THE ACT of creation finished, Henry stared as the little man with a round gold belly ran over to him as though coming home, which he supposed it was considering he'd rarely let the watch out of his sight since his grandfather willed the heirloom to him.

The mechanical stopped in front of Henry, its whole form radiating upstanding character much like Henry's grandfather and nothing like the menace of the other Natural's creations. The little man tipped a hat in greeting. It took Henry a moment to recognize the small circle of silver. He'd thought it safely stowed away in another pocket.

Henry knew he should be revolted, that his grandfather's gift had been destroyed, but the sight of the little man arrested his thoughts. The watch somehow resembled none other than his rather eccentric grandfather as impossible as that seemed.

It brought back memories of whispered stories told at bedtime when no one else was about. Stories of how his grandfather had hidden fugitives beneath his workshop during the religious purges so the noise of the bellows and forge would mask any sounds they might have made. Of all the people Sam could have brought to mind with this creation, she had chosen the best one to focus Henry on his true purpose, rather than the one crafted by assemblies filled with men who had never suffered hunger in their lifetimes.

If the law could trap someone like Sam, if a Natural raised with love rather than fear could be a person and not a monster, then the law was wrong. The law created monsters instead of protecting the people, a process as wrong as those who would lay down judgment for how a person spoke to God.

Henry lowered his free palm to the floor and waited for the mechanical man to climb onto it. A laugh burst from him as the mechanical looked from the palm to him and back as though questioning Henry's sanity. This creature wouldn't be the last to make that inquiry, but after a moment, it accepted the invitation, judging Henry sound in intent at least.

AT HIS laugh, Lily knew it was all over.

Samantha had gone from an innocent under his protection to a prize the moment she released the mechanical to walk on its own. He'd begun counting the awards he would claim for capturing a wild Natural by himself.

Her sister had finally moved enough for Lily to slide out from beneath. She braced her hands in front of her, twisted, and began to crawl toward him, the movement awkward with her ankle still in his grasp. Lily ignored the pain from her wrenched knee.

Henry glanced at her and released her ankle as though he'd forgotten he still held her.

Lily swallowed a gasp as the pain sharpened then eased, her full concentration on the man before her.

"Take me to the station, Henry. Charge me with hiding her. But if you have any love for me at all, put Samantha on a boat to the Continent. There are places on that shore for Naturals like her. Places where she won't be locked away as if she's a danger to society. You know she's not. You know that. Claim she escaped while you were securing me. Please, Henry. Don't do this to her."

His head began to shake even before she finished her plea, and Lily's chest ached with the pain of it. If only she'd knocked him harder. If only Samantha were aware enough to run now while Lily held his attention.

But neither of those were true, and so she'd lost everything.

"I've seen Naturals."

It took a moment before Lily realized Henry had spoken.

"I've seen them, and they're nothing like Sam. I've met her before, remember? Met and spent a pleasant evening here. If not for her finding my grandfather's watch I would never have guessed."

Lily flinched at the reminder, but Henry only lifted the hand that still held the little man. He stared at the mechanical for a moment with his head tipped to one side much like Samantha did when contemplating a puzzle.

"She no more belongs in one of those institutions than you should go to prison for keeping her safe from that."

She heard his words, but they made no sense. Lily could not match them to the man she knew, and yet they were exactly what a caring, intelligent person like him should see.

"But what of the law? I know you, Henry. You are a good man with a good reputation. I know how important upholding the law is to you."

Henry gave her one of those smiles that used to delight her. Now it helped her breathe again. He didn't have to say another word for her to know he would let them escape.

She scrambled to her feet, casting her gaze about for the bundle she'd tossed down when she ran to prevent this. "We'll leave," she promised. "Just let me pack up some of Samantha's things, and we'll go so far away that you won't have to lie for us. It'll be like we were never here at all."

Henry laughed again, but this one held a touch of sorrow Lily understood all too well. She paused long enough to run her fingers down his firm cheek and wished with all her heart the world were different.

Henry caught her hand against his face, the first time she'd touched him on her own, and if she had her way, the last. He hadn't anticipated how much her words would hurt, but he could not imagine a morning without seeing her, hearing her voice, teasing a smile to her lips.

He pushed half upright until he reached his knees, lowering the little man to the ground once again to free his other hand. "Have you forgotten why I came to you so formally dressed? What I said to you earlier?"

Lily tugged against his hold, but he would not free her hand, at least not until she listened to him.

"Of course not," she said after a pause. "But it changes nothing."

"That's where you're wrong. It changes everything. Sure, Sam isn't what I thought of her, but she's still a delightful piece of you, the first of many if I have any say in the matter."

The softening in her expression gave him hope.

Though he didn't want to break eye contact for fear Lily would find that an excuse to run, he glanced down to the little man now standing guard next to his knee. "Sorry, but I have a better use for this," he said as he snagged the mechanical's hat. The automatic apology to something that should have no concept of manners gave Henry pause, but he suspected it would become a common enough event if he could only get Lily to agree.

She had not moved an inch while he performed this office, though how she could with him keeping as tight a hold on her hand as he had her ankle, he didn't know.

Henry gave her a rueful smile that provoked one of her own before settling his features into a serious cast.

"I love you, Lily. I love how you truly care for those around you, how you can take command as well as the finest general, and how you would risk everything—reputation, even life—to help others. I want to spend the rest of my life aiding you and getting you out of trouble as need be."

He tugged their entwined hands until he held hers pressed to his heart. "I want to share in both your joys and your burdens—not that a child as wonderful as Sam should be considered a burden." Fumbling a bit, he placed the ring, of late the mechanical man's hat, onto her finger. "The Stapletons pride themselves on helping people and doing what is right—which is not always the same as what is law. I lose nothing in claiming you, and gain both the woman of my heart and a foothold in the Stapleton history to pass on to my sons."

"Sons?"

Her voice came out faint, and she pressed her free hand to her lips as though to recall the words.

Henry only grinned up at her. "Yes, sons, and more daughters, too. Say you'll accept me, that you feel the same. I never wanted a family before I met you, but now I cannot imagine living my life without both you and Samantha at my side."

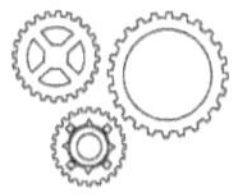

LILY STARED down into his striking blue eyes, absorbing the love in his intent expression. She began to shake her head before he'd even finished. "We can't stay here. I won't have your life turned upside down on account of us. You're a well-respected man. People count on you. You uphold the law for everyone. It's bad enough that I have to ask you to let us slip away in the night. I won't destroy your life and everything you believe in no matter how much you try to pretend it isn't so."

She jerked her hand away and tried to pull the ring off, but her frantic tugging only made it fit more firmly.

Henry caught both her hands as he rose to tuck her against him. "You're not listening to me. That ring wants free of you no more than I do. It's been in the family for generations, every one of which would be honored to have you and your daughter among them. We Stapletons believe in what's right. That's the principle I follow. Caging Sam for making an amusing toy is so far off the true path as to be criminal. She poses no danger to anyone or anything."

Lily twisted to get free, but all she managed was to lean far enough back to see his face. "You won't be so generous when it's something more important to you, though I'd think the loss of an heirloom watch would burn." She glanced down to see the mechanical man standing almost at attention nearby. "Sam doesn't ask, and she can't control it. When the fever takes over, she just...well... changes things. She says they cry out for the new form." Lily turned to see her sister had pulled out the other mechanical man to tinker with. Henry's watch, in this form or the previous, had made its preference clear.

Henry caught her chin and turned Lily to face him again. "I can live with it if you can. There's no possession more important than the people in our lives." He paused, his gaze turning inward for a heartbeat. "But you're right that we have to leave."

The emphasis on "we" left Lily no room to doubt he meant to join them.

"I'll take you to the Continent if that's what you wish, but I may have another option."

Lily stared at him, her mind whirring much like a mechanical man's gears as she realized he truly meant what he said, and nothing would sway him from this path.

"Go on," she whispered when it seemed he waited for something from her.

"I inherited my parents' estate along with the title I never wanted. I didn't have much use for it before, but it should be perfect for what we need now. It's a respectable size, the staff is trustworthy, and it's far enough in the country that my neighbors don't have all these newfangled mechanisms to tempt Sam. And should she lay claim to something unwittingly, it's unlikely to be irreplaceable. The estate can be a haven just as much as some place on the Continent that you've never seen. I'd like to think my presence would make it worth your while."

He quirked one eyebrow at the last, and Lily's mouth curved up in response.

She looked at him, really looked at him, for the first time since he'd proposed. The honesty and confidence that first drew her to him shone through as strong as it ever was. That he spoke the absolute truth could not be doubted. He was serious. Henry would happily throw away everything he'd worked for and retire to the country estate he'd so far avoided, just so he could be with them—with her.

A laugh bubbled up inside Lily as daydreams became an impossible reality sweeter than any pastry she'd ever made. "I don't understand how you can walk away from all of this, but yes." When Sam grew older and longed for more company would be soon enough to consider the Continent. For now, it would be enough to live together once again, with Henry at their side as her sister had suggested.

"Yes?"

She went up on tiptoe to lay a brazen kiss on his cheek. "Yes, I accept your proposal, for marriage, and to provide a home for myself and my sister."

"Your sister?"

Lily laughed again, amazed at how easily it came to her now that her burdens were shared. "Yes, my sister. I was but fourteen when she was born."

Henry caught Lily against him and swung her around in a circle. Then he bent down to whisper against the curve of her ear, "And yet you've been mother, protector, and friend to her ever since if I'm right in my guesses. I ask only that you be as strong a friend to me. I could not imagine someone more appropriate, more suited, to be my perfect mate."

"Can I fly, too?"

Lily twisted to the side to see Samantha had abandoned her toy to join in what she clearly thought to be a game.

A glance at Henry showed no sign of annoyance as he held out both hands to her little sister. "I can only spin one of you at a time, so I guess it's your turn after all. But first I need to ask you a question. Will you come to live with me in the country, you and Lily both?"

Sam glanced at Lily first before turning back to Henry with a grin. "Yes." She thrust her hands forward to renew the game as though the outcome had never been in question.

Henry's gaze, when it met Lily's over Samantha's head, was full of such joy she almost cried at the love she saw there. Her lips moved to form the only reply possible: *I love you, too.*

EPILOGUE

Henry had convinced Lily to return to the bakery until they were married to keep her reputation intact. No one else knew the truth, and he aimed to make sure it stayed that way.

He'd already started the arrangements, and with no parents on either side to object, they'd be married properly at his estate in a few days' time. They could explain away the haste as a need to get settled when he'd been away from his home so long.

Until then, Lily had Mr. Cooper to speak to, and Henry had his own confrontations to work through.

His discussion with the inspector went smoothly, the man half expecting this conversation since Henry inherited his father's title.

"Surprised it took you this long, Stapleton, or is it Lord Something or Other."

Henry waved the question off as he stepped out of the inspector's office. He had never seen a purpose in using his title at the station before now. He would not begin as he left its familiar walls for the last time.

"What's this we hear of you leaving?"

Fitz ambushed him the moment Henry entered the common area, but the other four were close behind.

"Got tired of slumming with us working folk?" Jim added as Henry moved to a table before answering.

Henry looked from one face to another, seeing a mix of disappointment and resignation in their expressions.

"I've spoken to the inspector. Parson will be heading the team, and you'll have your pick of the new recruits to fill out your number. I expect you to carry on as we have been. All people deserve the same protection, not just those—"

"Like you." Peter's interruption held a measure of disgust. "I never figgered you for liking the easy life."

Ken nodded as well. "Even I wouldn't have figured this."

Henry struggled to come up with an explanation they would accept, one that would not reveal the truth.

"Leave off your badgering," Fitz said. "You may not have figured it, but I knew this was coming, didn't I, Parson? It's the girl."

A flush heated his cheeks, but Henry wouldn't waste the rescue. "It's true. I have asked Lily to be my wife. We will be moving to my estate, though I suspect you'll catch sight of me from time to time. I have plans to use my title for some of the same aims we've upheld here."

Parson slapped him on the shoulder hard enough to rock Henry. "About time you got some use out of the fancy lettering. Take those pretty ideas of yours right into the law books. We'll be eager to see them put about proper like."

They all laughed at that, somewhat of a relief for Henry, but he had one more thing to say, something he'd been thinking about since the moment Lily agreed to become his wife.

"I have high hopes I'll change some things that you'll have to help the people accept. Not all we think we know is the whole truth."

Fitz gave him an odd look, but he wasn't ready to elaborate so the man shrugged. "Congratulations on your approaching nuptials then. May you find all the bliss a man can ask for."

"I guess this means no more buns," Jim muttered before joining the others in their well wishes.

Henry laughed. "Is that all the good I am to you lot? Then you should have no difficulty carrying on without me."

The protests his joke brought forth offered satisfaction that he'd made an impression in his time among them. "I'll miss each and every one of you as well. And to show my appreciation, I'm off to Cooper's Bakery right this moment to bring you some of those buns you have grown so accustomed to."

Parson laughed and shook his head at that. "As if you wouldn't seek out any excuse to go see your lady." Then his expression sobered, reminding Henry of the last time they'd discussed his interest. "You're a good man, Sergeant Henry. I always knew you'd do right by her."

Henry rose to leave, tossing back over his shoulder, "Well I remember the confidence you laced into your threats," as he went, leaving gales of laughter to follow him. He'd miss the station and his team, but he had a feeling his future would hold more adventures and good times than anything he left behind him.

A NOTE TO READERS

Thank you for reading *Safe Haven*, the prequel to The Steamship Chronicles. I hope you have enjoyed the tale of Lily's and Henry's romance. The series, beginning with *Secrets*, focuses on Samantha some eight years later when she meets Nathaniel Bowden, a cabin boy with big dreams. Together they face danger and adventure in a wild steamship voyage.

Would you like to know when my next book is available? You can subscribe to my newsletter to be kept up to date at my site:

www.margaretmcgaffeyfisk.com

Can I enlist your help in spreading the word about *Safe Haven* and my other works? The best way to do so is through writing a short book review and posting it on online retailers, reader sites, or on your blog. I appreciate all reviews, positive or negative. All I ask is you give your honest opinion.

If you'd like to read excerpts from *Secrets*, Book One of The Steamship Chronicles, and *A Country Masquerade*, Book Two of Uncommon Lords and Ladies, a sweet Regency romance series, please continue reading.

SECRETS

BOOK ONE OF THE STEAMSHIP CHRONICLES

Sam had been working on one of her machines in the garden when her sister's maid came to collect her.

"Lady Stapleton calls for you," Kate said, looking at the machine with a narrowed gaze.

Abandoning her tools, Sam leapt to her feet and grinned, pausing only to give the machine a quick pat in farewell.

Lily and Henry had been gone for a full week this time. The winter's chills had taken a toll on her sister's health and so Henry delayed his business until she felt well enough to travel. He took Lily on his trips whenever he could, weather permitting, and her sister seemed happier for the time away from the worries of the estate.

Still, she missed them when they were gone.

"You walk proper now." the maid said sharply before Sam could burst into a run.

The woman seemed to have a sixth sense for when Sam might misbehave and took every opportunity to scold. She'd treated Sam like a feral child even before the maid's copper-link necklace got caught up in one of her bouts.

No matter how much Sam had tried to explain and apologize, the woman continued to glare whenever Lily and Henry could not see. She'd returned the necklace with its broken clasp repaired, but that made no difference. Even fixing the steam generator so their piped water wouldn't freeze in the winter had failed to soften the maid's attitude.

It took all of Sam's focus to keep to a steady pace, but Kate's annoyance couldn't dampen Sam's growing excitement for all the maid schooled her walk.

"Now don't you be tiring your sister, Miss Samantha. She doesn't be needing any of your antics," the maid said when they came to a halt in front of the sitting room door.

Sam ignored the warning as she waited for Kate to sweep into the room first, a subtle breaking of tradition the woman used to put Sam in her place without drawing Lily's attention. But the maid only turned the silver knob, pulled the door open, and waved for her to enter.

Ducking her head to hide a cheeky smile, she stepped past Kate and into the room, anticipation wiping out the maid's unpleasantness.

"I'm so happy you're back." The words burst from her before she even looked around. "What did you find for me this time?"

Henry and Lily had gone to Dover, a full day's carriage ride from the estate. Lily always brought something back to make up for Sam's inability to leave, and ever since Henry set up a little workshop, those gifts often included small mechanical objects crafted by black-smiths. Only the most complicated and well-used machines would make her lose control, and she so loved working with the devices.

Sam's gaze found the empty sofa with its elegant, carved wood legs, the table bare of anything, and finally, her sister on the stuffed armchair, looking even more frail than usual after her winter sickness. But color highlighted Lily's cheeks, streaks of red Sam knew meant a secret waiting to burst out.

She crossed to her sister and knelt before the chair, her lanky height taller than Lily's when seated. "What is it then? I know it's got to be something special with you all colored up." Sam could hardly keep still as expectation triggered sparks of pleasure to dance along her nerves.

Lily still said nothing, the faint smile dropping from her expression. She put a hand on the top of Sam's red curls but did not move at first.

As always, her sister's presence brought with it calm enough to ease even the worst of Sam's episodes before something disastrous occurred. She leaned into the touch, enjoying the attention as Lily stroked her hair. But soon the quiet made her antsy.

"Hush, Samantha. Just sit a while."

If anything, the soft words made her more uncomfortable, especially with her sister's use of her full name.

Lily rarely did nothing.

She always had some work in her hands.

Sam had been growing steadily, and Lily often mended old clothes for the servants' children when she'd finished Sam's, one of the many reasons all of Henry's staff loved her. The table should have had her sister's latest project scattered across it, whether a crochet napkin or some clothing in need of repair.

Instead, it stood empty.

"I can't," Sam said after a pause. She pulled out from under her sister's hand and went to the sofa, folding her legs under her in a posture that usually made her sister scold.

Lily didn't even notice.

"It's a baby, isn't it? That's why you've been going to Dover with Henry, spending so much time away. That's what Cook says."

Sam refused to repeat Kate's speculations. Lily would never put a new child over Sam. They belonged together.

A faint smile touched Lily's mouth before she shook her head. "What have I told you about listening to the servant gossip?" As usual, the words held no heat. Lily understood better than anyone how much Sam craved company, even if it meant spending time in reach of the lady's maid and her barbs.

Her sister did not deny the gossip, but neither did she confirm it.

"That's not why I called you here, Samantha."

Tension rippled down Sam's back. Twice her sister called her Samantha when Lily knew she preferred Sam.

Lily twisted a strand of long blond hair between her fingers, looking anywhere but at Sam.

She tried to remember what she could have done to bring lines to Lily's face, but nothing came to mind. She'd even transformed a rusty old plow into a contraption to keep herself inside the workshop if she happened to feel a fever coming on while Lily was away. She didn't want her sister to have to worry.

"It's not about the plow, is it? Surely no one cared that I used it. Why the grass had grown up all around so I had to cut it free."

A laugh burst from Lily, leaving a comical expression in its wake as though her sister had not expected to find humor in the story. "You cut a plow free? And dragged it back to the workshop by yourself, I'd guess. It's not like Cook would have helped you…or Kate. Tell me you haven't co-opted one of Henry's workers? He needs them to keep the estate profitable, not running after your schemes."

Sam flushed and jerked her legs forward so they draped over the edge, her twisted skirt barely reaching her ankles and failing to hide the dirt-smeared feet below. "Old Mister Simmons is nice enough, especially after the steam generator, but he keeps the others away from me."

Lily shook her head. "Maybe better one of them than on your own after all. Someday you may regret your boyish ways."

Sam sat straighter, hands pressing brocade on either side of her. "What's the point in being a lady? It's not as if anyone's going to come courting. They don't know I'm here. Nor will I have a coming out. Not even in the Merchanter Ball as you would have if Mother had lived. My prison's larger now, but it's not much different from that old barn. I can't leave, and no one comes to see me either."

She remembered Kate's admonishment a bit too late. Front teeth sank into her lower lip as she stared at Lily.

Sam had never spoken so in her whole life. She hadn't even known the continued strictures bothered her until right then.

Lily's pale features became drawn, and she half-rose from the chair as though coming to cuddle Sam like years before. "If things could have been different …"

She drew on the calm Lily's earlier touch had produced as she prepared to wash away the hurt in her sister's expression, but Lily never gave her the chance.

"That's actually why I called you here." Her sister settled back, shoulders curled with an invisible weight. "Do you remember how it was before Henry came for us? Do you remember our plans?"

"Safe haven." The words came out in a reverent whisper, too strong a dream for even Henry's generosity to squash.

Eight years had passed, but the memory of sitting on a pillow of moldy hay as Lily described what awaited on the Continent rose sharp as though yesterday. Lily had read accounts from their father's journals telling of a place where Naturals gathered without a care for who saw them transform a simple machine into the mechanical that lived at its heart. They spoke of a place where Sam would have friends, people around her who never once wore that look of fear her abilities brought forth. Even Cook, who had befriended Sam for her enthusiastic appetite, still kept a wary eye out for any sign of an approaching bout.

It had been a beautiful dream, something to keep a little girl warm at night as Lily worked herself almost to death earning their passage when they had only rumors to guide them after the crossing.

"But instead we came here." Her voice went flat when she'd intended to show Lily that she held no regrets.

In truth, most days the estate offered enough room to ramble and the workshop gave her the ability to play with her natural affinity to machines. If she didn't have many friends—only one really beyond her family—at least she didn't live in fear that her smallest slip would cost her everything, and worst, cost Lily. Only lately had disquiet rippled beneath the peace Sam had found here.

Kate's sour words had struck hard. Sure, neither Henry nor Lily showed any sign of resenting her presence, but neither had they filled the empty rooms with the children both had wanted. Now Sam had to wonder if the choice lay not in chance but in the same fear that hovered in the servants' eyes when they thought Henry couldn't see.

"Yes, we came here. And it's better for you than that old barn for sure, but wouldn't you want something more? You talk of Merchanter Balls, so I'd guess you've been haunting Henry's library again, but you can never have that here."

Lily rose, her skirts swirling down to tiny feet encased in slippers. "Wouldn't you prefer a place where you could follow your nature without restraint? Where you didn't have to watch your every instinct?"

Sam had never thought her sister unkind before.

She stared at Lily, mouth half open. "Of course I would," she said, jerking to her feet, "But it's not possible. It never was no matter how much we pretended. I try not to think on it."

A wistful smile crept across Lily's face. "I thought I'd taught you how important it is to have dreams. Sometimes that's all we have."

Anger melted away as Sam crossed to her older sister, noticing for the first time how they stood almost the same height despite more than ten years between them. "You did, and it's true. But we found our dream of a safe haven here, with your Henry and my workshop."

Lily shrugged and turned half away. "It's not enough. It never will be with you still trapped. You said so yourself."

Sam stared at her dirty feet, the earlier anger turned inward. "I didn't mean it," she said to her big toe. "I wasn't thinking."

A strangled laugh brought Sam's face up again.

"It's when we don't think that the truth comes out, and a surer truth I've never heard from your lips. Whether you admit to it or not, the confinement chafes. It has since you got over the delight of grass beneath your feet."

Sam crossed the toes of one foot over the other in a feeble attempt to hide the grass stains that always seemed present, wishing she'd stopped long enough to put on the slippers her sister preferred she wore.

Lily only shook her head. "You might have put the Continent from your mind, but I've had Henry make discrete inquiries since you turned thirteen. There's more to life than running wild in a cage. You deserve that as much as anyone, and the accounts in Father's journals prove there's something to find."

Sam barely heard anything past the fact that Henry had kept searching. The dream came back with the full force of longing, a vision of the two of them in true freedom now grown to include Henry's strength. "Has he discovered something?"

When Lily glanced away, Sam's shoulders slumped. There had been nothing despite Lily's hopes. She'd figured that out years ago, though she'd never let on.

Her sister straightened her spine. "He has found it."

The soft words took a moment to sink in. Tingling swept through her limbs, and her scalp tickled as the dream became reality.

Around her, the room broke into its component parts, metal highlighted in her vision and a mantelpiece clock she desperately ignored every day called out for mobility.

"You're old enough now to go on your own."

The rest of what Lily said hit with the force of a blow, silencing the aether-driven pull from the clock and everything else.

"My own? What of you and Henry? Why can't you come too?" Sam's voice spiraled up until it sounded much younger than her fifteen years, but she couldn't help the desperation in its tones. "We're supposed to be together."

The way Lily had avoided Sam's eyes now gained another meaning.

Her sister pressed both hands to her stomach and slumped into the chair. "We were supposed to be together, Samantha. Father asked me to keep you safe, and I have. But I can't give you what you need any longer. It's cruel to keep you here when I know there's a better place for you to be."

"Yes, a better place. But one with room for you as well. Like we'd always planned it." Sam grabbed Lily's fingers and laced them through hers. "Together."

Lily pulled free. "My place is here with Henry." Her voice trembled on the words.

Sam relaxed, sensing the weakness in her sister's argument. She had only to press, and Lily would give in. Her sister would let them stay together as they were meant to be. "Henry can come too. I'm sure there's a place for him on the Continent. Who wouldn't like your husband? It would be perfect." She reached for the hand again.

Lily pulled out of reach then raised her fingers to rub at her temple. "Henry belongs here. He has roots going back generations."

Sam stared at Lily. She couldn't believe her sister would even think such a thing, much less plan it.

Lily's expression didn't change. Her sister didn't laugh and reveal this to be a jest. The pain shining from her eyes showed the decision hadn't been lightly made, but made it had been.

"You really mean it. Just like Kate said." Sam took a step back toward the door. "You are going to cast me out. You have your normal life here with Henry, your trips to Dover, your hateful lady's maid. Why do you need a dangerous little sister who can never leave?"

She twisted and stumbled from the room, vision clouded with unshed tears.

Lily called her name, but Sam didn't stop. She couldn't.

A COUNTRY MASQUERADE

BOOK TWO OF THE UNCOMMON LORDS AND LADIES SERIES

Lady Barbara Whitfeld stood still as Sarah helped her out of the simple, but elegant, white gown she'd worn to the poetry reading.

She hardly noticed Sarah's efforts, her mind still caught up in the rich tones and lovely words Aubrey St. Vincent had offered in his reading. He'd put the rest of the gentlemen to shame.

"Your mother should not be having you out so late every night," Sarah scolded. "You'll have to sleep well past noon to keep from getting dark circles beneath your eyes, and what then will the young gentlemen say."

Barbara laughed as cloth pooled about her feet. "Sarah, you sound like a woman twice your age. You know full well you'd have been happy at my side. You're just jealous." She stepped free and sat at the dressing table.

Her best friend and maid softened enough to smile. "Jealous of what? Listening to conceited men talking about lines on paper? I think you're mistaken."

"Ah, but what lines. To hear them read aloud makes such a difference. Resonate tones, elocution…it makes the poems come alive, I tell you."

Sarah released the last of the pins holding back Barbara's riot of dark brown curls and ran her fingers through to loosen them further. "He was there, then, was he?"

Barbara raised both hands to cover her cheeks, but from Sarah's knowing glance reflected in the mirror, she knew she'd failed to hide her response. She shrugged as though it were of no consequence, then a grin burst out across her lips. "Aubrey St. Vincent. A better specimen of the male breed I've yet to see. Handsome, reasoned, and kind. The perfect gentleman."

"You'd have me believe him a paragon of virtues. The only man to meet such a standard is one still in the cradle, and even then they're all about demanding attention." Sarah laid a heavy stroke through Barbara's hair, and it caught on a tangle.

"Not so rough," Barbara cried. "And he is all that and more." She raised a hand to count off on her fingers. "He escorts his youngest sister to all manner of gatherings when other young men are off seeking their own pleasures. He doesn't retire to the card room the moment they arrive at an event. He's willing to participate when asked like tonight, though he had no plans to read. One of the readers fell ill and could not attend. Then there's how he considers education in philosophy something even women should be able to strive for."

"Enough, enough," Sarah wailed, both hands pressed to her ears though the twinkle in her eyes belied her protests. "You've made quite a study of the man, but I've heard it all before. You marked him as your interest at the very start of the season. So tell me, did you speak with him this time?"

All confidence drained from Barbara as she stared at her twisting fingers, no longer raised to count his worth. She'd encountered Aubrey on her first outing when, sitting against the wall unnoticed, she'd overheard him discussing how unsettled the Continent was. His conversation attracted her attention when the other young men spoke only of fashion and horses.

Since then, his presence acted like a beacon, calling out to her. She did what she could to be within earshot, and if she succeeded, almost every time she learned something new or had a thought to ponder. Still, she'd never spoken a single word to the man.

Sarah tucked a curl back behind Barbara's ear. "Your mother would be happy to arrange an introduction, I'm sure. He's a man of good standing, from a good family, and with a title of his own free and clear since he has only sisters. An earl, he'll be."

Barbara pulled away and rose, though what she intended once upright, she had no idea. "I've seen the way mothers bring their daughters up to meet him. He's surrounded by them too often for me to miss. I can't come to him as just another young lady in white and expect him to notice."

"Don't you think that way," Sarah said, rushing to catch her arm. "You meet with him proper, Barbara, or you'll do nothing but make yourself out to be a fool, especially when the man in question shows no sign of returning your regard. But then, how could he share your interest when you've avoided the chance for an introduction. You want to stand out from the rest. That's how to do it. Get your introduction and show Lord Aubrey you can put more than two sentences together without dissolving into cloying giggles."

They shared a significant look, remembering the afternoon party Lady Whitfeld had arranged shortly after Barbara's presentation. Sarah had assisted the staff and so suffered the same babble and attempts to preen Barbara had. A bunch of ninnies with nothing of consequence between their ears, and her mother wanted her to find bosom friends among them.

Barbara had Sarah for her companion. None of them had offered an adequate substitute.

Her mirth faded as she addressed the flaw in her approach. "But what if I do? What if, when faced with none other than the most perfect Aubrey St. Vincent, my tongue curls up in my mouth and my mind vanishes into the clouds. Sarah, how can I be sure of the impression I'll give. You've heard my mother often enough. She says first impressions are the most important as they form the foundation of everything going forward. I cannot chance this going astray."

Sarah shook her head, but when she met Barbara's gaze, her own held sympathy. "Better to take that risk than never to chance at all. Trust yourself enough. You've certainly studied his habits, read whatever you heard him mention, and even plagued your father about the questions you didn't understand. You've prepared for this moment better than most gentleman study for their examinations. Besides, how could he not be taken in by your combination of beauty and thought? If he isn't, then he's not the paragon you seem to think him either."

Barbara laughed at Sarah's stout support, but knew she'd be hard pressed to put her friend's advice into effect when faced with the gentleman in question.

"Just promise me you'll try nothing foolish. Tradition has set these ways for presentation to society, and it's because they prove worthwhile. Hatching some crazy plan will only bring you trouble."

Barbara turned away more to hide her smile than because she disagreed. "You're sounding old enough to be my mother again, Sarah. Not so long ago, you were happy to join me in whatever adventures I could concoct."

She climbed into bed, pulling the covers up under her chin so she could peek out at her friend.

Sarah paused in collecting the discarded clothing. "Fair enough," she said, her gaze on a distance place, "But that was when you were at your father's country estate, or your uncle's farm, not here in London. You're not to run wild. It will do you a disservice and break your mother's heart. If sounding old is how I must be to keep you from trouble, then I'll turn the hag rather than see you receive a reputation you cannot recover from."

Barbara sank lower, no longer playing as she accepted the somber warning. London did have its own standards, and gossip ran rampant. She'd taken many months to adjust when brought up from the country a few years ago, and even now found its strictures confining.

"Besides," Sarah added with a rich chuckle, "If you fail to catch in your season, you'll be left to live out your days under your mother's thumb, which means I will too. That's a sorry end neither of us would prefer."

Though her mother little deserved such a slight, and well Sarah knew it, Barbara appreciated the effort to lighten her mood. She waved her friend off with a smile. "Then I'd best catch some sleep or those black circles will come whether you will them or not."

Arms full with soiled clothing, Sarah paused in the doorway. "I'll bring you a cup of chamomile tea. That will send you into a deep, soothing rest."

Her friend didn't wait for Barbara to answer, and from the yawn that split Barbara's face, she suspected sleep would overtake her long before Sarah returned. At least the tea would not go to waste, and Sarah needed the rest as much as any what with having to manage Barbara's complicated wardrobe now that she'd been presented.

Thoughts full of balls, readings, and theater, Barbara sank into oblivion. At least in her dreams, she could amaze Aubrey with her wit and wisdom.

ABOUT THE AUTHOR

Margaret McGaffey Fisk is a storyteller whose tales often cross genres and worlds to bring events and characters to life. She currently writes steampunk, romance, science fiction, and fantasy but will go wherever the story takes her. Foreign Service brat, data entry clerk, veterinary tech, editor, manager, and freelance programmer are among the roles she's lived, giving depth to the cultures and people that form the heart of her works. As her website is titled, she offers tales to tide you over.

She'd love to hear from you through any of the contact points listed on her website, or you can subscribe to her newsletter for release announcements, snippets, and other news:

www.margaretmcgaffeyfisk.com/subscribe-to-my-newsletter

ACKNOWLEDGEMENTS

Safe Haven is the prequel to a steampunk series I've been working on for a while. It was originally written as a novella for a steampunk anthology call from Entangled Publishing. As odd as it may seem, I'd like to thank Kerri-Leigh Grady who sent me a rewrite request with specific feedback. In doing the work, the novella grew too long for the proposed line, but her suggestions helped make *Safe Haven* into the novel you have just enjoyed.

My husband, Colin Fisk, as proofreader, photographer, and overall support team, deserves a huge dose of thanks for all his hard work and tolerance of all of mine. Valerie Comer; my mother, Elizabeth McGaffey; my sister, Deirdre McGaffey Schwein; and the rest of my family also contributed to bringing *Safe Haven* to you through beta reading, cover art suggestions, and work on the marketing text.

As you can see, though I'm taking this indie journey, I am not walking it alone. The last piece of my publishing process, and the last essential group, is you, my readers. Thank you for allowing me to bend your figurative ear and for welcoming my characters into your lives.